I0715250

BOYFRIENDISH

Carol J. Roth

Copyright © 2024 Carol J. Roth
All rights reserved.
ISBN: 978-1-7331407-8-2

For my amazing family that supports me in everything I do. Anitra, Neil, Astrid, Vee—I love you.

CHAPTER ONE: CHRIS

"*Mister* Quinn!" The voice stops me in my tracks, and the tone makes me think this is probably not the first time she's tried to get my attention. I turn reluctantly, arm still raised dramatically—my impassioned rendition of "Kill the Wabbit" from an old Bugs Bunny cartoon had just reached a dramatic crescendo—to see the vice principal glaring at me.

I lower my arm and lay it across my stomach for an exaggerated bow, but the few kids that had paused to snicker while I sang have already moved on, and there's just Mrs. Banks, looking even more irritated.

"Is that your attempt at comedy?" *Ouch.* What would she know about it anyway?

"Trying my best." I grin wide, wondering if you can be taken to the principal's office just for singing cartoon opera at the top of your lungs.

Luckily, she seems to have no interest in pressing the matter. "Save it for the talent show," she says, and makes a shooing gesture with her hands. "Just get to the assembly. And from now on, try and keep your ... comedy ... to a dull roar, okay Chris?"

I think about standing to attention and snapping off a salute but settle on a mumbled "okay" and slinking away.

The auditorium is already more than half full by the time I get there, but it's easy to spot Marty by his mop of curly hair and the stupid poncho he wears almost every day. I've tried to get him to stop by telling him it's the most cliche thing a pothead could wear, but it never works. "Yeah, but it's like wearing a blanket," he said once. "It's like I never got out of bed!"

I fling myself onto the seat next to him and he jumps a little, like he might've been half dozing. "Oh hey Chris," he says in his unhurried way.

"Sup, Marty?" I pull an apple out of my backpack and hold it up. "Wanna split this with me?"

Marty looks like he's considering the logistics of sharing an apple, then shrugs. "Sure, man." I don't think I've ever heard him say no to anything I've asked him unless it seems like it might require a lot of extra effort from him.

I've been waiting all day to show off the trick I found online. I cup the apple in my hands with my thumbs close together and squeeze. It breaks perfectly in half and I hold up the two pieces triumphantly. "Wow!" Marty laughs and takes one of them. "Is this a Honeycrisp?" he says appreciatively as he crunches on it.

"I ... have no idea." Marty is the most random sometimes. Who the hell knows what kind of apple they have? But he's always a friendly audience for whatever jokes or tricks I'm working on, and he never seems to get annoyed with me, which puts him in about one millionth of one percent of the world's population.

I bite into my half of the apple and look around. It's only October, so the school year feels pretty new; it's still kind of a novelty to be around this many other people. By Christmas break it'll feel like we've been stuck together forever, and when the end of the year approaches, everything will feel stale and I'll be dying to get to summer break and do my own thing. Even if my own thing mainly involves a lot of sitting in Marty's basement watching old movies and eating chips and salsa ... which'll make me antsy to get around a bunch of people again by the end of summer. It's a sad cycle, but hey, at least I'm self-aware.

The room is getting louder as more and more people file in. Everyone's just so happy to have an excuse to skip sixth period and hang out with friends instead. I'm missing Algebra II, which I actually weirdly sort of enjoy—not enough that I wouldn't rather be goofing off in the auditorium, of course.

The biggest source of noise is a group of football and hockey players in the back, who are obviously trying to keep the attention of a cluster of girls nearby. It's like watching a nature documentary; I imagine some old guy with an English accent narrating. "The males of the species use loud noises and aggressive movements to demonstrate their virility to the females they hope to mate with." The girl that most of them are trying to impress, of course, is Cherri (pronounced "Sherry," though naturally a lot of guys mispronounce her name on purpose so they can make gross jokes).

She indulges the attention-hungry jocks with the occasional roll of her eyes or bitchy smirk but seems more interested in whispering with her friends—I think of them as the "mean girls," which I know is a stereotype, but I can't help it. They just are. I bet most schools have a group like them—it's how a cliche becomes a cliche, right? At least Cherri is somewhat progressive; her little clique also includes a guy. But "mean girls and one boy" doesn't roll off the tongue the same way, so "mean girls" it is.

I finish my apple and stick the core in a side mesh pocket of my backpack, hoping I remember to take it out before it goes bad. I look over and reach out for Marty's, only to see the last of his half of the core disappear into his mouth. I shake my head in disbelief but he doesn't seem to notice, just crunches methodically, lost in thought. Weirdo.

An amplified voice rings out. "Attention, everybody!" It's the principal, Mr. Carson, standing at the podium on stage. The din of babbling voices gradually quiets down enough for him to start. He goes through a feel-good spiel about how great the first semester has been so far, blah blah blah. That's an awfully blanket statement; I mean, some people are probably having a great year, mine's been kind of neutral, and then there's Abby Spelchik, whose whole year is going to be defined by the starting-her-period-while-wearing-white-pants incident. But whatever; I know Mr. Carson is just saying what he's supposed to say.

With that out of the way, he launches into another boring speech about the value of taking part in extracurriculars. That's the reason for this assembly, he explains: to learn about the many "amazing and enriching" clubs and activities and "encourage participation."

Everybody's zoning out by the time he finally stops talking, and then the leaders of all the groups come on stage one by one. Most of them are super awkward and really bad at public speaking, but at least they get cheers from their friends, some a lot fewer than others. Having the chess club follow cheerleading is just, wow. I guess they're going in alphabetical order? But it doesn't matter to me anyway; I can't stay after school every day even if I was interested in any of the groups.

A few more go by and I lose focus entirely, sneaking a glance at my phone, hiding it behind my backpack on my lap, as I'm positive at least half the audience is doing. But I catch a teacher giving me side-eye like she might come over to check on me, so I turn it off, slip it into my backpack, and try to look attentive.

A girl walks up on stage to slightly louder cheers than the last few speakers, looking more confident than a lot of them too. She's short and kind of skinny, dressed in all black. Her long curly hair is dyed black with dark blue streaks, piled up in a loose bun.

She steps up to the podium and pulls the mike down to her level. "Hey, I'm Jemma." There are several more whoops and screams and she smiles. "I'm the co-chair of the Genders and Sexualities Alliance."

I've seen her a lot in the halls and lunchroom, but I've never had any classes with her; I think she's a senior. I find myself thinking she's cute, though I guess she's gay. Not that that changes my chances with a girl one bit. I'm completely and utterly incapable of even thinking about making a move or telling a girl I like her.

I had a quasi-dating thing with a girl named Harriet in middle school that confused me for the entire time it lasted—which was all of two weeks. It was kind of like what I'd imagine an arranged marriage would feel like; her friends and my friends decided to push us together constantly and not leave us alone until I asked her to "go with" me (for some reason, that's what everyone called dating in my middle school; I'm in my third year of high school and no one *ever* says that here). She said yes, but I think she was as confused as I was. I never knew for sure, because we only saw each other around groups of giggling friends, so it's not like we could have a real conversation ever. Luckily, her friends got bored with the situation and made up a reason she should get mad and dump me. And that's the short and pathetic story of my entire love life.

It's kind of depressing all of a sudden, looking up at the cute confident girl on stage and thinking A) she's gay and B) I'm hopeless. She's talking about a new event her club is organizing this year, the "first ever Hennepin

High School queer prom." Which, again, I'm not even planning to go to *regular* prom, or homecoming for that matter, so it has nothing to do with me. I turn my attention to whispering stupid things to Marty to try and make him laugh, which honestly isn't very hard to do but is a fun way to pass the time.

It passes even faster than I realize, because the end of school bell rings right in the middle of some guy's presentation. He looks up from his notes, shrugs, and yells over the sudden commotion of people starting to talk and get out of their seats: "So join the Video Game Club!" That gets a few laughs.

The principal takes his place at the podium. "Students, students!" he shouts. Everyone stops what they're doing and their babble dies down. "Looks like we've run out of time, but be sure to look into the Yearbook Club, Young Democrats, and Young Republicans. Some great stuff, uh, going on in those clubs. All right, you're dismissed."

"Okay, I'm sold," I tell Marty as we gather our stuff and head toward the doors. "What a brilliant pitch! I'm going to join Young Democrats *and* Young Republicans."

"Yeah, man, maybe you could, like, help them settle their differences." Marty chuckles. "Hey, you wanna come over and play games?"

"Nah, I can't today. See you at the car." I almost always drive Marty to and from school; I've been doing it ever since I got my parents' old car for my sixteenth birthday last February. We go our separate ways to our lockers. As I round a corner, I spot Cherri and her cluster of hangers-on. I keep my head down as I get closer to them. Even though they've done nothing to me, I always feel a little wary around them.

"I just think it's fucking pathetic, like a cry for attention or whatever," I hear her say. Another girl pipes in, "Yeah, like queer people can't go to *our* prom? Hello, last year's prom queen was trans!" "Maybe the Video Game Club is gonna want their own prom next," a third girl helpfully adds, which causes giggles.

My eyes land on the sole dude in the group—Benji. I know him from my English class, and plus he's rich and popular, so everybody knows his name. He looks slightly uncomfortable about the jokes, even though he's smiling, and I feel bad for him, because I think he's gay and it seems like pretty inconsiderate stuff to say in front of him. He looks back at me for a second, then past me, like he didn't even see me there. That's just how everyone in the group is, though. It's like they barely recognize the rest of us are humans. My momentary pang of sympathy passes just like that and I keep going.

CHAPTER TWO: BENJI

"What's your deal, girl?"

Cherri's glare jolts me out of my daze. "Just ... tired," I say lamely. We're in the parking lot by her car, which is parked between Alicia's and Tiara's, as it is every day. It's getting a little chilly, but it's still a nice enough day that we can wait outside the cars.

Everly is sitting on the hood of Alicia's car eating pork rinds—don't ask me, I couldn't tell you what's up with that—and texting, I'm assuming with a guy since every female friend she has is right here. Val and Alicia are playing with filters on their phones or something.

Cherri and Tiara are cracking themselves up by coming up with creative insults for girls in their classes—a never-fail way to pass the time.

"Well, don't you think it's perfect?" Cherri demands, still glaring at me.

I have no idea what I missed but I suck air in through my lips and whisper, "Brutal." Right answer. She smirks and moves on to her next victim. "What about Jean?"

"Who?" Tiara gives her a blank look.

"You know, The Count." Cherri's biting her lip to hold back her laughter.

"The what?"

"The Count. From Sesame Street. You know." She looks at me and I oblige with a half-assed impression.

"Ah ah ah. Vun vunderful pork rind. Two vunderful pork rinds. *Three—*" I shrug and drop it. Meanwhile Cherri's scrolling through Instagram, and she stops and shows a picture to Tiara.

"This bitch." Tiara nods in recognition and Cherri scrolls a little more. "See? *See?*" She sticks her phone in front of Tiara's face insistently. "When she pulls her hair back she looks *exactly* like The Count!" She and Tiara lose it, scrolling through Jean's feed and squealing with laughter every few seconds, I'm assuming whenever they come across another pic of her in a ponytail.

"Wait! Stop!" Tiara thrusts her finger at the screen. "*Oh* my god. Look at this one. *Why* would she post this? Does she think her ass is actually hot? It's *so* not. It's like an atrophied Black girl butt! Like, big, but not in a good way. Big and droopy." That's it, Cherri is done for. The two of them are crying into each other's shoulders with laughter.

I don't know why, but this whole routine isn't as funny to me as it usually is. I lean against the side of Cherri's car, wondering when we can leave. Well, not until Ben and Dante come out, I know that already.

I see Jemma Matthews coming out of the school, walking with Monica Parsons, the other leader of the GSA, and I feel my stomach tighten up. I find myself hoping none of my friends spot her and get back into their weird issue with the queer prom idea. It's not like they were saying anything homophobic, but there was something hostile about the way they were talking. And I don't know how to feel about the sense I got that, when they were kind of othering queer people for wanting "their" own prom to compete with "our" prom, they thought of me as an "us," not a "them."

"Oh my god, I keep forgetting it's my birthday next month," I say loudly. That gets my friends looking at me and hopefully not over where Jemma and Monica are.

"Shit, girl!" Cherri says scoldingly. "Why didn't you remind us before now? Are you having a party?" That starts a whole burst of excited chatter about when and where I'm having a party, and my stomach, which had just started to relax, seizes up again. Of course, this is exactly *why* I haven't been talking about it, and I regret my impulsive decision to use it as a diversion to keep them from trashing some queer girls I'm not even friends with, really, anymore, and their dance that I'm not even interested in.

But it doesn't matter now. What's done is done. Cherri's sunk her teeth into this idea like a vampire on a virgin.

"We have no time," she announces. "We've got to get started planning *now*. You'll have it at your place, right?"

I quickly sift through the other options. I mean, what? Chuck E Cheese? Pump It Up? The bowling alley? I suppress a sigh. "Yeah, I guess." I remember my dad's got an out-of-town trip coming up soon. "My birthday's on a Thursday, but if we have it the Saturday after, that should work."

"God, *finally*!" Cherri slaps my shoulder with pent-up excitement. "I've been *dying* to have a party there. It's going to be so *hot*!"

"It can't be really big though," I say hastily. Even though there's no danger of my mom being disturbed by a loud party—she falls asleep with the TV turned up loud in their bedroom when my dad's not home—I want to try and keep this thing I accidentally set in motion from getting out of control. "My place is really small, remember?"

"Small?" she practically snorts. "Yeah sure, it's a small *entire* fucking house!" She wheels around to the other girls. They're all agreeing eagerly except Val, who's relatively new to our group and probably hasn't been there, but even she looks intrigued.

"Oh my god, and it's so *clean*," Cherri adds. "I have *never* seen any of these bitches' rooms as clean as you keep your place. It's like gay boy magic or something."

"It's not magic, it's our cleaner," I argue. I guess I'm not in the mood for any more commentary from Cherri about queer stuff, even if it's a harmless compliment.

"We *all* have cleaners," Tiara breaks in. "But none of our rooms stay clean all the time."

Alicia agrees. "The second they leave it's like—" she mimics the sound of an explosion and spreads her hands out "—a makeup and shoe bomb exploded."

"And your walls are like—" Cherri shakes her head in admiration. "You're like a minimalist or something. Every time I hang out there, it makes me want to tear down all the pictures and random things I have in my room when I get home."

"Yeah, that's true!" Everly says, like she's just made an amazing discovery. "And, like, how do you not have any random toys or kid shit like stuffed animals still hanging around? I have never seen one single thing like that. With my room, I'll do like a big clearout every few years, and I *always* notice more baby things to get rid of."

Luckily at that point Ben and Dante come out, and everyone focuses on piling into the three cars so we can go to our usual coffee shop. Ben gets in with Tiara, and Cherri gives Dante a ride, and the rest of us know they each want a little privacy, so Alicia takes Everly, Val, and me in her car.

It's kind of a relief. Cherri and Tiara are definitely the big *big* personalities in our group, so when they're not there, the energy is a lot more mellow. They can be so exhilarating when we're having fun, but on a day like today when I'm feeling a little off, it's nice to just sit with my other friends and be on our phones, commenting occasionally on whatever we happen to be watching. The car ride is just that, and I'm feeling more normal by the time we get to the coffee shop.

Which helps me cope when Cherri launches right back into it, as if she hasn't just spent a car ride getting felt up by the school's star quarterback. The vampire always needs more life blood.

"So who are you going to invite?" she asks. "I mean, like, especially?" That gets everyone's attention; there's a sudden hush. I shrug, starting to feel uncomfortable again.

"It's Lance, right?" Everly asks, and my cheeks feel a little warm. I glance at her to try and figure out what she's thinking. "I get it, girl, it's all right," she says. "He's hot as shit. We had fun, but that was last year. I'm not, like, permanently banning him from dating other people."

It's pretty cool, actually, her saying that. A lot of people get weird and edgy about people they've dated dating people they know, and I can't imagine most girls would be so blase if a guy they were seeing hooked up with another *guy*. God, I imagine Cherri would castrate both of them. With her eyes. Her rage would give her castrating superpowers.

But I shake my head. "We're not really—" I feel everyone's eyes on me and sigh dramatically, pulling my hair back with my fingers, then laugh. "God, put me on the spot. I don't know, okay? Lance is great. I just wouldn't say we're dating exactly."

No, I don't know what you'd call what I'm doing with Lance. It's like one minute he'll be looking really deep into my eyes and I start to get butterflies, and the next he's telling me he's still trying to figure out if he's into guys. I'm like, hello? Are you into *me*? Or am I just some test subject for the big experiment of figuring out your sexuality? We've made out a few times and, like, he's *so* gorgeous and a pretty good kisser—*and* a senior *and* a hockey player—but somehow I don't feel any, like, *heat* coming from him. And wondering if he's even turned on at all is a big turn-off for me, so I've felt a little less into him every time we get together.

Also—it's hard to admit this even to myself, because it makes me feel shallow for still somewhat liking him—he's really just kind of deeply ... dumb. He seems to *want* to be an intellectual, so it makes it even more cringey when he tries to say something deep or meaningful and it's either really stupid and obvious or it makes no sense whatsoever.

For example. When he was talking about turning eighteen soon the other day, he told me that he wants to vote "the most liberal there is" and he wished there was just something that told him who to vote for so he didn't have to think about all the different political races. I mean it's one thing to be apathetic; he was trying to be the opposite of that and tell me how concerned he is about all the "liberal stuff" and managed to sound like the most ignorant, apathetic guy ever.

So, I don't know. Something's gotta give if I'm going to keep messing around with him—

he's got to either stop saying such stupid shit or start kissing me like he actually wants to be kissing me. Preferably both, but it's not like I have a ton of options that are—well, to be honest, that Cherri would approve of someone in her group going out with. The gay dating pool in our school is already smaller than the straight one, but for me, it's miniscule.

I realize I've kind of zoned out again, but Cherri doesn't notice this time; she's already busy making the guest list and figuring out who's going to get the drinks and pot. At least I won't have to put in much effort planning this party I didn't want. My main job will just be keeping a handle on things and making sure it doesn't go too overboard.

CHAPTER THREE: JEMMA

Even from the stage, I could see my friends' reaction when I announced it. Disbelief, triumph, excitement; even Monica, who has such low affect that she can look kind of blank, had her mouth dropped open. She almost looked accusing as I left the stage and went to join her and the rest of the GSA in the seats. I just had to shrug and whisper that we'd have an emergency meeting after the assembly.

We pass the word in whispers to the board. We don't have roles like president, treasurer, secretary, and stuff, because we don't divide the work that way. Instead we have a board of directors. Monica and I were both equally second-in-command last year when Nick Rosen was board chair, so it ended up that people wanted us to be co-chairs this year.

After the assembly's over, we find our teacher sponsor Ms. Lyons and ask her to let us into the English classroom we use for meetings. As soon as we have the room, everyone starts squealing and hugging and talking at once.

I explain how Mr. Carson pulled me aside right before I got on stage to let me know our petition for a queer prom had finally been approved and a date set for early January, after winter break—so it wouldn't clash with the Valentine's dance or prom, he said. So I didn't have a chance to tell the rest of the group, but I just had to make the announcement on stage, since when were we going to get another chance to talk in front of the entire school like that?

We celebrate for maybe five minutes: thinking big about the event, imagining what it's going to mean for our group's visibility and especially for closeted or questioning students.

Soon, though, the excitement starts dying down and we kind of collectively face the realization that we've been approved to hold a schoolwide dance but only been given about two months to plan it. Yikes.

"Okay, wait," I say, holding up my hands, when the excited babble turns to worried questions. "Here's what we're gonna do. Everyone go home and make lists of what we need, what you can bring, what the school could help us with, stuff like that. We'll use our regular meeting next week to really get into planning together." I look around and smile in what I hope is a brave way. "Go team queer?"

That's become kind of our silly catchphrase this year, so it gets everyone laughing and looking more relaxed. There's a chorus of "Go team queer!" and then Monica shoos everyone out so Ms. Lyons can lock the door and go home. The teacher congratulates us again as she leaves, and there's another round of celebrating in the hallway. Then everyone starts to drift away and it's just Monica and me left standing in the hallway.

"Well." She shakes her head. "Wow."

"I know." I'm still a little dazed myself.

"I get why you sent everyone home without, like, full assignments, but you and I really do need to start planning today if we're gonna pull this off," she says, almost reproachfully.

"You think?"

"Positive." Monica's always positive about everything she thinks—and usually right, which is pretty annoying.

I suppress a sigh. I've been trying to avoid situations where we're alone this school year, but it looks like I'm ending my streak as of right now. "Okay, but we have to do it at my place—it's my night to make dinner." My mom and I are super busy and on different schedules, so we mostly just fix quick meals for ourselves, but she tries to find two nights a week we can eat together, and we take turns cooking.

We grab our jackets from our lockers and head out to the parking lot. Monica walks me to my car, which feels a little awkward because it reminds me of last year, when we were dating and I drove both of us to and from school, but instead of holding hands and talking we're walking side by side without touching, in silence, seemingly having both forgotten how to do small talk all of a sudden. When we get there, she pauses by my car like she's waiting for something, but I just unlock it and start to get in. "Okay, see you at your place," she says, and walks away to her car.

I toss my backpack into the passenger seat and let out the sigh I've been holding in. *This is fine*, I tell myself. We've got to figure out how to be friends or at least friendly acquaintances so we can run this club together.

The first month or so of GSA meetings this school year was excruciating, Monica either looking sadly at me or making cutting little comments about me being cruel or commitment-phobic or whatever; just being generally unconstructive and making everyone including me uncomfortable. Of course, everyone had already elected us as co-chairs (by unanimous vote) before they fully realized

A) that we'd broken up and B) that Monica was going to be such a downer about it. I think once they realized B, they felt too bad for her about A to even suggest removing her from her position, so we were all stuck just trying to work around her self-pity.

The past few weeks, it's finally felt like she's getting over it and looking happier (or at least more normal). Unfortunately, along with that change, I sometimes get the feeling she's flirting with me, trying to get things going between us again. It could be all in my imagination and, even if not, it's easy enough to ignore when we're around other people. Taking her home, hanging out alone together, feels, I don't know. Fraught. Fraught with tension, fraught with peril, all the fraughts.

I spot her car behind me a few times in the rearview on the way, and she pulls up behind me in front of my place. Mom and I live in the top left corner of a quadruplex, so there's not enough room in the back driveway for all our cars. Except when they need to plow snow or clean leaves, parking in the front is much easier anyway.

Inside, Monica leaves her shoes on the little mat by the door, and I try not to notice how she adjusts them to be perfectly lined up and perpendicular to the wall. She hangs her fall coat up, smoothing it unnecessarily.

I go straight to the kitchen to start fixing dinner. I'm making hummus, and it always tastes better if it sits for a few hours in the fridge, so I start pulling out ingredients. Monica sets her laptop up on the island.

"Where should we start?" I open cans of chickpeas and dump them in the food processor.

"Well, we have to figure out decorations, and food and drink … music—that's a huge one—teacher chaperones? Is that our responsibility?" She types furiously. "We'll have to check."

"What about selling tickets?" I break in. "Regular prom requires tickets, right?"

"Right." Monica looks thoughtful. "We'll need to ask about that too. It'd help cover costs and maybe we could donate anything left over to a good cause."

"One of the biggest things is making sure everyone knows it's an inclusive event."

"Yeah, if someone gets up in arms about a queer-only prom, that could just be a disaster."

"It's not just that. We need to make sure people, especially like freshmen and sophomores, who aren't ready to come out can still come to the dance. You know, incognito."

"That's really smart." Monica's typing busily.

"What about publicity?" I smash some garlic cloves and add them and other ingredients to the food processor. "There are some cute things we could steal from movies and stuff to build hype, but we'll have to plan them fast."

Monica's fingers fly on the keyboard as she takes down my thoughts, peppering them with her own. Ideas pour out as I blend my hummus and scoop the thick, semi-smooth results into a bowl with a spatula, cover it with plastic wrap, and put it in the fridge. I'd forgotten how well we work together. "Hey, can you help me chop veggies for the wraps?" She smiles and nods, and I can't help but think she looks cute in the glow from the setting sun, her precise bangs and bob looking softer, the light revealing the little hairs that rebelled against her perfect hairstyle and curled up here and there over the course of the day.

I set out two cutting boards and knives and we work on cucumber, pepper, Romaine lettuce, and tomatoes. Monica finishes slicing some red onion and gets a small bowl. "If I soak these in ice water, it'll cut down on the aftertaste."

"Thanks for helping." She smiles, wipes her hands, and comes over to me.

"Of course," she says softly, tucking a loose curl behind my ear. I know this is a bad idea; I can feel that it is, but it also feels so peaceful and kind of romantic, the scent of fresh vegetables and the quiet house to ourselves and the pinkish sunset coming through the windows ... before I know what's happening, Monica's kissing me, holding my face in her hands, and I'm leaning into it a little, the thought of how wrong it is lost in the pleasure of the moment.

"I've been thinking," Monica whispers against my neck as she kisses her way down it.

"Yeah?" I murmur it softly, reluctant to say anything, as if the sound of my voice will bring me back to a reality where this shouldn't be happening.

"I'm driving up north to visit a couple colleges this weekend," she says. "If I got a hotel room, maybe you could come with and we could hang out?"

The spell is definitely broken. She starts to trace her lips back up toward mine, but I stiffen and push her away. "Monica, stop."

She pulls back reluctantly, her lipstick a little smudged, instinctively smoothing her hair. "Why?" she asks bluntly. "Jemma, I miss going out with you. We're so good together."

I shake my head, unable to talk about what snapped me out of thinking that was okay. I'm just glad something did.

"We can't go back," I tell her sternly. Seeing her burgundy-stained lips start to tug downward at the edges (not again), I relent a bit. "I'm sorry if I led you on just now. I wasn't thinking. But this isn't what I want."

Monica takes a breath and straightens her plaid skirt and cardigan. "I gotta go." She packs up her laptop and barely says goodbye.

After she leaves, I put the cut veggies in containers and stick them in the fridge. My heart is pounding like I narrowly missed getting hit by a train or something, but my stomach feels hollow with guilt. I sit down with my sketch pad but can't think of what to draw, so I fill a page with scribbles and random geometric patterns, trying to calm myself down before Mom gets home.

CHAPTER FOUR: CHRIS

The smell of Grandma's beef stew is unmistakable. I'm not even sure she uses all that much seasoning in it so I don't know why it just triggers this nostalgia thing in my brain when I smell it, but it does, even faintly through the cracked-open kitchen windows of their little house.

It's getting a little darker, but the sky is this orangey pink that seems like it makes everything the light touches glow with some kind of magic. It adds to the feeling of nostalgia.

Grandpa must be feeling it too, because when I find him on the three-season back porch (after I give Grandma a kiss in the kitchen), he's got his little Bluetooth speaker I got for him last Christmas playing oldies from the fifties and sixties. I recognize Ricky Nelson's voice right away. My family got Grandpa an iPad a few years ago and I helped him set up a streaming account. After a lot of avoiding using it unless I made him, and grumbling about how hard it was to understand, he's come to use it much more than the ancient little CD player and stacks of CDs he used for years.

I make sure to open and shut the door noisily as I come out to where he is. If he's somewhere else mentally and I sneak up on him by accident, it can turn his mood sour for the rest of the visit.

Luckily he's not so out of it that he doesn't hear the door. He turns and gives me a big smile. "Well, howdy, Chris!" he says in a fake drawl. Relief washes over me. He's having a good day.

I figured if it was really bad, Grandma would've warned me, but I don't like to be like "How's he doing today?" before I go see him. It makes it feel like he's, I don't know, something to be scared of. But I never quite know until I see his face.

"Hey Grandpa," I say loudly over the music. He turns it down a little and I give him a hug where he's sitting in his ancient brown leather armchair. It used to be a recliner but doesn't work anymore, and Grandma spent years trying to convince him to let her get rid of it and buy new living room furniture. They finally compromised and now it lives on the porch with a bunch of other mismatched furniture, getting more cracked and faded little by little.

He smells like the shaving cream he's used my whole life, and I notice his chin is smooth with only a couple of small nicks where there's a dot of dried blood. He's having a *really* good day!

He asks me about school, so I show him my new trick with the apple and tell him it's the most valuable thing I've learned all year so far. He laughs and tells me about the time in fifth grade he decided the best way to impress the girl he liked was to bring eggs to school and juggle them while the teacher's back was turned. He didn't realize (until he dropped it) that one of the eggs was rotten.

I've heard the story about a million times, but it honestly is funny every time. Grandpa's a great storyteller and his description of his teacher (as well as his impression of the look on her face) always cracks me up.

"So I'm glad you picked a safer way to impress girls," he says at the grand finale of his story. "Was she impressed?"

I laugh and make a face. "That's not why I did it, and anyway, I don't think that's how you hook chicks nowadays. Especially since I'm in high school, not fifth grade."

Grandpa shakes his head like he's disgusted. "'Hook chicks.' Kids these days." He slips into a Humphrey Bogart impression; I've seen plenty of those old detective movies with him so I know it right away. "In my day we called 'em 'dollsh,'" Grandpa Bogart slurs. "We'd go 'Hey, dollface, wanna shee me juggle these rotten eggsh?'"

"That's right, I forgot. And you wore fedoras back then, even in fifth grade, right?"

"That'sh right," he agrees. "And carried a flashk of whishkey wherever I went."

"The good old days." I nod nostalgically.

"The good old days." He stops his Bogart impression and looks a little sad, so I change the subject and ask if he wants to play Scrabble. Soon we've got the ancient board set up on the glass-topped picnic table and I'm sitting in an old dining room chair across from him. A song by The Coasters comes on and I find myself singing it under my breath as I look for a good play with my crappy letters. I know way more fifties and sixties songs and movies and pop culture stuff than someone my age should, just from hanging around Grandpa.

Grandma brings in some coffee for us—it's weak Folgers or some crappy brand, and at this time of day I know it's decaf, but I'm used to it. She stops by Grandpa's chair and puts an arm around his shoulders, then bends down to kiss the mostly bald top of his head. He leans back against her and they stay like that for a minute, eyes closed, both with the same little smile on their faces.

After she leaves, Grandpa suddenly looks conspiratorial. "Say, did you get what I asked you?"

I almost forgot, even though I put them in my backpack after school. Before that, I'd stashed them deep under my car's front seat, tucked in with fast food wrappers and other trash, convinced my parents would find them, but I lucked out. I unzip my backpack and pull out a two-pack of cigarillos.

Grandpa's eyes gleam. "We better go out back." He jerks his head toward the door. "She'll smell it if we light it in here."

This is all feeling like a really bad idea, but Grandpa's been asking every time I've seen him recently—every time his mind is clear, anyway. It's funny, Marty and I don't have fake IDs, but the guy he buys pot from does, so he paid him a little extra to pick these up for me. I can't tell Grandpa that I had to go to a drug dealer to get him his Swisher Sweets, which is too bad—it's the kind of funny story he'd appreciate. I think he'd believe that I wasn't the one actually buying drugs or dealing with the guy directly, but what if he let something slip accidentally to my parents or my grandma? That'd be a whole other thing.

So I keep quiet about that and help Grandpa out of his chair and down the back steps into the yard. We walk slowly, me keeping close to him to catch him if he trips or gets light-headed, until we're by the garage.

After a guilty glance at the windows to make sure Grandma isn't watching, I pull the pack out and try to hand it to Grandpa. But he shakes his head and steps back. "I can't touch 'em; she'll smell it on me a mile away. I need you to smoke one for me and I'll just enjoy it from here." He moves a couple more feet away.

"Grandpa!" I'm honestly shocked. "I can't *smoke*. I don't want to get addicted, and plus what if Grandma smells it on *me*?"

"Just don't get too close to her when you leave." His voice takes on a teasing tone. "And you ain't gonna get *addicted* from one cigar; you don't even get much of a buzz off 'em. Just don't make this a habit, okay?"

Shaking my head, I open the packet and take out one of the cigarillos. I vaguely remember Grandpa smoking them when I was little, but I haven't seen one in years and never held one. I turn it over, then pull out the pack of matches I brought. "How do I do this, anyway?"

Grandpa instructs me on lighting one end while I suck on the other, warning me to only breathe it into my mouth, not my lungs. The warm bittersweet smoke coats the inside of my mouth and I almost cough even though I do manage not to inhale too deep. It's a bizarre experience; I never planned to smoke, and when I heard about peer pressure during all those anti-drug school lessons, I never pictured it coming from my own grandfather. I mean, he was the kind of guy who'd give me sneaky sips of his beer at family barbecues and stuff, but this seems a bit extreme!

But he looks so happy, standing a few feet away from me, breathing in the smoke wafting his way, that I indulge him for a few puffs. He looks small and frail when he's upright, seeming to sway a little on his feet, his white hair (what's left of it) standing on end in the slight breeze.

Even though it's only sitting in my mouth for a couple seconds, the smoke makes my gums tingle and my heart beat faster. Not a great combination with my nerves already being on edge thinking about getting caught. "Okay, I can't do this anymore," I tell Grandpa, and he lets me put it out.

I scrape it along the cement of the back driveway until there's no hint of anything that could cause a spark and then drop it into the garbage bin. I tuck the matches and the packet containing the other cigarillo into my pocket with a plan to stash it in the same place in my car again. I'd rather not repeat this whole undercover routine, but I'll hold onto it just in case Grandpa insists on it again sometime.

I realize it's starting to get dark already, and I still have homework to do, but we head back to the porch and finish our Scrabble game. He wins, of course. As I'm putting the letters away, another song comes on and he turns it up. I recognize it, though I can't remember the name of the group.

You can dance
Every dance with the guy who gives you the eye
Let him hold you tight

You can smile
Every smile for the man who held your hand
'Neath the pale moonlight

"God," Grandpa says, "this one takes me back." He closes his eyes and taps his thigh, off tempo, joining in on the part that really rings a bell for me: "But don't forget who's takin' you home and in whose arms you're gonna be." His singing voice is raspy and a little flat. "So darlin', save the last dance for me." He opens his eyes and smiles at me. "This was one of our songs, me and your grandma, back in college when we were still just going steady."

It's sweet, but I try to imagine my grandma dancing with another guy before going home with Grandpa and I can't do it. I giggle, suddenly picturing her at a club with a bunch of college students but Grandma's the age she is now, with her gray hair and the sweatpants she usually wears around the house. *Get it, Grandma!* I think, and that makes me laugh more. When she pokes her head in a minute later to tell us dinner's ready, I lose it.

She gives me a look somewhere between amused and annoyed and tells me to help Grandpa to the dining room table, but he asks if he can eat out here. So she goes back to the kitchen to fix him a bowl of beef stew, and I take the opportunity to slip out so I don't have to hug and kiss her and maybe get in trouble for the smoke smell on my jacket and breath. (I plan to chew some gum and change my clothes right when I get home, so hopefully my mom and dad won't notice either!)

Grandpa's expression is starting to look a little more vague, which happens a lot as it starts to get late, but he's still nodding along to the song when I give him a quick hug, scoop up my backpack and make a break for it.

CHAPTER FIVE: BENJI

The halls are pretty much empty as I trudge to my first period classroom for English. I'm so late already it's not really worth running. Besides, it's not like there'll really be any consequences; the school will robocall my parents about my tardiness, I'll make up some excuse about Cherri having car trouble, and nothing else will happen. Maybe some ding in the great cosmic school record or something, but not enough to make a difference in my grades.

Everly's parents are both doctors with early shifts, so her house is always empty in the morning. That's why it's our designated location for a wake-and-bake party.

We don't do them too often; we've all got college on our minds even though some of us are juniors. The sporadic tardies are no big deal; the challenge is getting my head back in school mode after smoking weed early in the morning. I've got the kind of high where I forget what I'm doing unless I concentrate really hard—which I sometimes forget to do.

I stop off at a water fountain for a long drink and to splash a little water on my face. Then, realizing I'm wearing a touch of foundation and eyeliner today, I duck into a boys' room to make sure it didn't run. I take some breaths and look myself in the eye in the mirror. "You got this," I say encouragingly. My reflection looks skeptical, but it's time to go to class before first period totally ends.

Mrs. Frenzi looks up, annoyed of course, as I open her door quietly and slip inside. "Sorry," I whisper. "Car trouble." I catch Val smirking a little bit and flash her a warning glance; she never comes to our wake-and-bakes because she doesn't like to smoke weed, but she knows all about them.

"I was just explaining our assignment, but you can review it in my daily email tonight," Mrs. Frenzi says, sounding unconvinced about my excuse. "It's a team assignment, so we've just finished choosing partners and then having the teams choose books. There's two books left and only one person left, um—" she heads toward her desk to check attendance, but someone raises their hand with a question about the assignment and she goes over to them.

I flounce into my seat next to Val, who's paired off with Cindy Mason. Good choice. Cindy's all business and never seems to mind doing most of the work for group projects. Still, I'm annoyed Val didn't hold out and pick me for her partner.

There's not much to do since I don't know the assignment, don't have a book, and don't have a partner, so I focus on staying still in my seat and not losing track of where I am. At last Mrs. Frenzi finishes explaining something to the team across the room and makes her way back to me. "All right, where was I?" she asks, half to herself. "Oh right, I was going to remind myself who else is—"

She doesn't finish her thought because her door creaks open again and someone peers around the corner before slipping sheepishly inside. *Oh great.* It's Chris Quinn.

"Ah, that's right." Mrs. Frenzi taps the attendance sheet. "And what's *your* excuse, Mr. Quinn?" I suddenly feel like teachers call him that more than they do other kids. Maybe it's an attempt to impose some kind of maturity on him from the outside, because he is one of the spazziest, most annoying kids in our grade. He's constantly doing something that's supposed to be funny but is actually just to get attention.

Right now, though, he's admirably not making a face as he holds up a slip of paper. "I have a pass from the princi—"

"Put it on my desk." Mrs. Frenzi is clearly tired of interruptions so late in the period. "You're the last one to class, so I'm not going through everything again; you can read my daily later. Long story short, you need to pick a partner for a new project. Your partner is, by process of elimination, Benji, and you two should agree on a book. There's two left." She gestures to a table at the front of the room under the whiteboard.

Chris looks over at me and I roll my eyes a little—I'm not even sure if it's at him or the situation—and get up from my desk. We stand side by side at the table, staring down at the two pairs of books on it. One is *The Picture of Dorian Gray* by Oscar Wilde, and the other is *Tess of the D'Urbervilles* by Thomas Hardy.

We each pick them up and turn them over like we're reading the back cover copy. I don't know if he is, but I'm not. Judging from the titles and pictures on the covers—Dorian is a blank-faced dude in a high collar and Tess looks worried and wears a long frumpy dress—they're both boring books about boring people in the 1700s or something, but to me there's no contest: *Dorian* looks like it's about half as long as *Tess*. Chris isn't saying anything, so I do: "How about this one?" I look at him and hold up the obviously thinner one.

"Sure, that sounds good," he says quietly. I'm not sure I've ever seen Chris Quinn say *anything* quietly and not in a funny accent. Maybe someone finally put him on Ritalin or something, or maybe he's having an off day. Whatever's gotten into him, I'm glad for it.

"What's the assignment?" he asks.

I shrug. "I missed it too."

As if on cue, Mrs. Frenzi comes over. "Ah, *The Picture of Dorian Gray*. Are you familiar with it, or Oscar Wilde?" We both shake our heads. "Well, he lived a very interesting life — and there's a lot of subtext in this novel. I hope you both enjoy the project."

I feel like she emphasizes some of her words a little more than necessary, especially "interesting" and "subtext," while looking right at me. Is she trying to give me a wink-wink nod-nod that the author's gay? Maybe I'm just being high and reading too much into everything, who knows?

Anyway, I still have no idea what the assignment is or whether we'll need to meet up after school. "I guess let's email each other once we find out what we need to do?" Chris nods. "Okay, well ..." I go back to my desk with my copy of the book and sit down just as the bell rings to let us out of first period.

In the hall, I confront Val. "What the hell? Why didn't you tell Mrs. Frenzi *we* were gonna be partners?"

"I tried!" Val sounds defensive. "She made everyone in class pick someone who was already there."

Before I can think of a reply, I see Chris dart out of the classroom then walk unsteadily down the hall balancing the book on his forehead, bumping into people who don't see him in time to move out of his way. Val and I exchange looks, and I shake my head. Of all the randos I could be stuck with, why Chris Quinn?

CHAPTER SIX: JEMMA

It's a slow day at the store, so I've got my
laptop up behind the counter, kind of flipping
aimlessly between a college application essay
that's mostly blank screen and the to-do list for
the dance, not getting anything done on either
of them. Between those two huge, looming
things and wondering where I stand with
Monica, my brain isn't sure what to worry
about first.

We haven't spoken or messaged since I
basically kicked her out of my place. At least
she sent me a copy of the notes she'd taken so I
can be somewhat prepared for our meeting

tomorrow. Still, my stomach's in knots, hoping I haven't accidentally brought us back to square one. I'm not sure the club can take more tension and distractions from the two people who are supposed to be leading it.

And my college applications are just … well, it's hard to concentrate on them with so much else going on. I wince at the first couple sentences of my essay and flip hastily away from it.

The bell of the front door is a welcome distraction. The guy who comes in is tall and skinny with hair that can't decide if it's curly or straight—or maybe it's just messed up from the wind. He looks familiar, though I can't quite place him. Maybe he goes to my school. I smile at him. "Let me know if I can help you find anything."

He gives a little wave and disappears into the stacks. I'd normally leave it at that, but the last thing I want to be doing is standing behind the counter with only my gigantic stressful school event, my non-responsive co-chair, and my incomplete college applications to keep me company. And he's literally the first customer we've had my whole shift. So I set my computer on a shelf out of sight and go toward the aisle he slipped into. I see him crouched down, looking at the bottom row of books.

"That wasn't just empty words." His shoulders jerk and he turns. I swear his face gets a little red; I guess he doesn't do well with jump scares. "About helping you," I clarify. "I can help you find what you're looking for. I'm bored as shit anyway; it's been dead today." I shrug. "I mean bookstores are dying in general, so it's not that surprising." I turn and survey the shelf behind me. "What are you looking for? Horror, sci-fi, fantasy?"

"No ..." He finally speaks, sounding tentative.

"Tender coming-of-age novel?" I tease. My eye falls on a book and I grab it. "If so, I recommend this. *Are You There, God? It's Me, Margaret* by Judy Blume. It might seem kind of tame now, but it was banned a lot for daring to talk about masturbation." I look at him and widen my eyes. "*Female* masturbation!" I cover my mouth as if shocked by the very idea.

If he wasn't blushing before, he's beet red now. It's kinda funny but I also feel bad for scaring the poor kid. I put the book down. "Not what you're looking for, huh? Well, what *do* you need?"

"I, uh, it's ..." His mind seems to have gone blank; he holds his hands up a few inches apart as if trying to conjure a picture of a book.

"A book about this size?" I mimic his gestures. "Yep, we've got quite a few of those but" —I sweep my hand to the side, indicating all the shelves around us— "you'll have to be a *bit* more specific than that."

"*Dorian Gray!*" he finally bursts out. "*The Picture of Dorian Gray* by ... Oscar somebody. It's for a class project. I lost the school's copy, so ..."

"Oscar Wilde," I correct him. "Now we're getting somewhere. Follow me."

"I, uh, was also hoping—" he stammers from behind me. "Is there, like, a graphic novel version of it too?"

I can't resist pretending to look disgusted. "Already planning to cheat before you even start the assignment?"

"No! I just—I'm a more ... visual learner? So I thought if I read them together it'd, like, help me ..."

"Calm down, I'm not the book police." I reach the shelf with the W's and pull one out. A portrait of a pale-faced, intense-looking man with dark eyes and cheekbones to die for stares back at me. "Here you go. I actually do think there's a graphic novel adaptation, but I don't think we have it in stock. Come on, I'll look it up for you."

He tags along behind me to the register like one of those baby chicks some science teachers give their students. I do some digging on the store computer and, just like I thought, we don't have any copies in the store. "I can order one for you and we'll give you a call when it comes in if you want." I lower my voice conspiratorially. "Or you can probably get it way cheaper if you buy it on Amazon, but, you know, support local, defeat the evil empire, et cetera." I smile and shrug. "So what do you think?"

He nods eagerly, his face starting to return to its normal color. "Yeah, uh, support local, that sounds good."

"Great!" I scan the regular version of *Dorian Gray* and he pulls out a crumpled twenty to pay for it. "Can I get your name and a phone number or email address? So we can tell you when the other book comes in."

"Oh, yeah, it's Chris. Last name Quinn." He rattles off his number and I type it into the system.

"Do you go to Hennepin?"

"Yeah, I'm a junior there."

I nod. "Me too. Senior though."

"I know." I look up and his face starts to darken again. He adds hastily, "I mean, I just saw you at the ... assembly thing the other day. You were on stage."

"Cool." So he knows I'm queer. I wonder if that's what's got him so flustered. Maybe he's weirded out by it ... or maybe he's in the closet. "You thinking about coming to the dance?"

He looks embarrassed. "I—I don't know. I guess dances aren't really my ... thing, but you know, it sounds fun." He looks around in a jittery way. "So, I don't know, maybe?"

Hard to tell from that reaction. I hand him his book. "Enjoy. It's a pretty good story. Oscar Wilde's cool, right? Kind of an O.G. gay icon."

That draws a blank look from him. "Oh, I didn't know! It was just one of the last books left to pick for the project." Okay, maybe he's just a regular awkward eleventh grader. I go back to my bookseller script.

"Well, anyway, someone'll give you a call when the graphic novel comes in." I give him a bright impersonal smile. "Have a great day!"

My welcome distraction leaves the store and I'm left to run out the remaining minutes of my shift alone, worrying and not getting anything done.

CHAPTER SEVEN: CHRIS

The doorbell rings and I feel a little bit of dread in the bottom of my stomach, but I run for it. "I got it!"

"Good; it's only ever Jehovah's Witnesses when I get the door," my mom says as I jog past the living room.

I wish it *was* them, honestly. I'm not looking forward to awkward one-on-one time with the lone boy of the mean girls clique. But I run for the door anyway because I don't exactly want him talking to one of my family members; we're all a little weird and I don't need him judging me for that. It's bad enough he's coming over.

And all because Grandpa took a fall the morning we picked partners, and Grandma couldn't reach anyone else so she called me to bring some paperwork and stuff to the hospital because she didn't want to leave his side. He ended up being fine, no broken bones or even a concussion, so all it did was give me a scare, make me late for class, and create *this* unpleasant situation.

When I read the English assignment it confirmed what I was afraid of, that we'd need to meet after school for it. Between us we have to write a short biography of the author, an essay about the book (we can choose symbolism, historical context, or literary context), and a "creative writing" piece. The teacher suggested a story that continues the plot of the novel, poetry inspired by it, or diary entries from at least two characters' points of view.

Benji and I emailed to set up a time to meet. I asked where, hoping he'd offer up his probably gigantic home and get to show off how rich he is. "Let's do it at your house," he wrote back, and my heart sank.

Hopefully I'm too unimportant for him to bother reporting back to his friends about my tacky house. My parents don't bother too much with aesthetics or whatever, so most of our furniture is worn out and mismatched. A long time ago, they went through a thing of putting up framed photos of me and my brother and sister, and then never took them down or replaced them. When I say a long time ago I mean I was about two years old. So that's what's on the wall leading up the stairs, me as a toddler with a big clueless grin on my fat face.

And it's Saturday afternoon so our house is at its messiest. We usually do what my mom calls "eliminate the evidence" on Sunday; she puts on a timer and we all run around tidying away as much of the week's accumulated mess as we can in half an hour. I like that they aren't super fussy about a clean house, but suddenly I wish they kept up on it a bit more than that.

Although some of the mess is mine, so that's kind of hypocritical.

It's too late now anyway, because here I am about to open the door to Benji Swenson, gay-boy mean-girl and son of local minor celebrity Wyatt Swenson, a TV news anchor and part of the Swenson family that made it rich on canned and frozen meat products. Benji's dad doesn't work for the company but somehow he's super rich from it? I don't get how those things work, but it means Benji is part of the upper crust of Hennepin High. I'm surprised he's not in a fancy private school, I suddenly think, right as I open the door. Maybe he likes feeling superior or something.

"Hi." I try for a neutral tone, hoping my face doesn't look bitter from what I was just thinking. The look on *his* face isn't too hard to read; this is the last thing he wants to be doing. *At least we've got that in common,* I think grimly as he says "hi" back and I stand aside to let him in.

I want to rush him to my room before he can see much of the rest of the house, but he stands for a couple seconds looking around. "My room is up this way," I say, standing at the foot of the stairs and waiting for him to get the hint. Finally he follows me, though as I turn at the top of the stairs, I see him looking at the super old photos on the wall. I get the urge to apologize, but what do I have to be sorry for? We can't pick our parents and their income or style (or lack thereof).

"I like your house," he says as I finally get him into my room.

"Oh, thanks," I say, even though I know he's lying. And what a weird lie to bother telling. "It's always kind of messy on Saturdays ..." There I go half apologizing; I'm annoyed at myself.

"It's nice." *Whatever.* I shut the door with relief.

I sit on my bed, which is already strewn with the book, a notebook and my laptop, and gesture at my desk chair. Benji sits and pulls his own stuff out of his backpack. I've shoved everything on my desk into a messy pile at the back, so he has room to open his computer and set his book down. Then he swivels the chair around to face me. "So have you had a chance to read it yet?"

"Most of it." I've gotten about halfway through. It's weird because it's like written in this stuffy language but the story is slightly creepy, about a guy who's kind of innocent and naive, but he's got this friend that's always pushing him to basically be selfish and immoral. He falls in love with this actress named Sybil, but when her acting sucks one night he dumps her and she kills herself. Oh, and he's got this painting of himself that starts to look evil the more bad stuff he does. That's as far as I've gotten.

"Same," Benji says. "Well, I started it anyway ..." He suddenly notices the brand new graphic novel sitting on the corner of my bed. I got a call first thing this morning that it was ready to pick up, so I drove over to get it before our meetup. Jemma wasn't working today, which felt slightly disappointing. She was sort of making fun of me at the bookstore, I know, but somehow it felt okay, like she didn't really mean it to be mean. I kind of liked her teasing, and she was even cuter up close. And knowing she's gay makes it feel safer to crush on her. It's nice knowing I don't have a chance but that, for once, it has nothing to do with what a dork I am.

"I just got this, so I haven't looked at it yet." I hand it to Benji. "Thought it might help me get through the real book if I had pictures to help me visualize it."

"Good idea." He flips through it.

I stand up. "I'm gonna get a soda and stuff. You want anything?"

"Um, Diet Coke if you've got one."

"Yep! I'll be right back."

I run down the stairs to the first floor and then to the basement. Our regular fridge is always crammed with food so there's another one just for drinks down there. I stop by the kitchen on my way back to my room, finding a bag of salt and vinegar potato chips and a package of Oreos.

Benji's deep into the graphic novel when I come back. I hand him his drink and set the snacks on the edge of the bed. "Just some crappy junk food if we need it." *Goddammit, why do I keep apologizing?*

"Nice." He doesn't look up. "This story is creepy, huh?"

"That's what I've been thinking!" I say. "I thought it was gonna be boring. I mean, it's a little boring, but it's better than I thought."

"Dorian's a baller." I snort with unexpected laughter, and he looks up and laughs a little too. Despite the fact that he looks so perfect in that way rich kids do—expensive-looking clothes, hair that's just the right length so it's always falling in his eyes and needing him to comb it back with his fingers—he doesn't seem as out of place in my room as I thought he would. Because he's not acting like he *feels* out of place, I realize; not all like uncomfortable and disgusted at me and everything around him, like I expected him to be.

"Really? So far it seems like Harry, or Lord Henry or whatever his name is, he's the real baller. Dorian's just kind of naive and confused." I gesture at the graphic novel. "You've gotten way ahead of me with that."

"Sorry I'm hogging it … I thought since it's yours, if I can just read through it fast now while I'm here, then you can look at it whenever?"

"Yeah, that's fine." I'm kind of flattered he's so interested in it. "I'll try to get a little farther in the actual book while you finish that, then maybe we can talk about what we should do for the assignment."

I read some more, and it's a little easier because that's what we're here for; when I'm just trying to read on my own I usually end up getting distracted and going on my phone or playing a videogame. I'm weirdly into Lord Henry, at least the way he talks. It's odd and wordy but fun to read.

"Done!" Benji closes the graphic novel and pushes it across the bed at me. "I mean, I skimmed pretty fast, but I caught most of it. Thanks for getting that."

"Yeah, no problem," I say. "So for the creative writing part, I was thinking we could do the diary thing? I could write a couple of entries from Lord Henry's point of view if you wanted to do Dorian or the artist guy—Bay-sil? Bah-sil? However you say it."

"That sounds good," Benji says. "I'll go with Dorian. The other guy just mopes around and eventually gets murdered. Plus we don't know how to pronounce his name." We both laugh again, and it's weird, but I feel like we're … getting along?

"Cool." I crack open the bag of chips and grab a handful, then hold it out. Benji takes a couple. "What about the essay part?" I say with my mouth full.

Benji holds a finger up, chewing and swallowing his chips before talking. Way classier than me, I think, but not with the same resentment as I would've felt before he actually came over. "I was thinking there's like, a gay feeling to this?" He adds hastily, "I don't just say that about everything because I'm gay, by the way." For some reason that makes us laugh really hard.

"But for real," he says, once he can talk, "I don't know if it's just the illustrations, but it feels like both of the other guys are kind of in love with Dorian? And like the painter wants to just, like, crush on him by painting him, but Lord Henry almost wants to destroy him? Or at least control him and make him do what he wants. But it feels like from the comic book that they're both hot for him."

I nod, my own laughter dying down. "That makes sense, now that you say it. They go on and on about his looks in the beginning, and it almost feels like Henry is flirting with him when he's talking to him. Plus, the girl at the bookstore told me Oscar Wilde is, like, a gay icon or something?"

"Really? Hey, maybe we could kind of make the whole project about that!" Benji counts the parts of the assignment on his fingers. "Like the bio will mention that, obviously, and our essay can be about the gay symbolism or whatever. And then maybe our diary entries could be the characters writing as if, like, Henry really is gay and in love with Dorian."

Uncharted territory for me, though it'd be nice to have a clear idea of what we're doing. "I've never written about anything like that, but I guess I could try."

Benji looks a little flustered, which I've never seen before. "Oh, I mean, if that seems at all weird, we don't have to do it. It was just a random idea."

It *does* seem a little weird, but the more I think about it, I can't think why it should be a problem. Plus, it suddenly occurs to me, even a rich popular kid like Benji is probably used to a lot of crappy behavior from people just because he's gay. Maybe I don't need to add onto that by acting like this is a problem. "Well, I'll try, but we'll look at each other's stuff and you let me know if I say anything really lame or accidentally offensive or something, okay?"

He looks relieved. "Okay, totally. Sorry to put you on the spot to write about stuff you don't know anything about."

"That's okay." The mood feels like it needs lightening, so I put on my best English accent and channel Lord Henry. "Those are the wages one pays when one chooses a perilous book like this for one's project." That sets Benji off on his hardest laughing fit yet; he's got actual tears in his eyes. I munch some more chips, grinning and feeling pleased with myself.

We talk a bit more, divvying up the bio and essay and planning to email rough drafts to each other. I feel weirdly comfortable around Benji—and way relieved that this wasn't the awkward unpleasant cringe-fest I thought this meetup would be.

As we walk to the front door—Benji holding a handful of Oreos for the road—I'm not feeling as weird about him seeing the rest of my house. We pause in the foyer while he puts on his coat and wraps a scarf around his neck; it's finally starting to feel more like Minnesota fall, unfortunately.

"Well, thanks for hosting, and for the snacks and all." He looks off to the side for a second, thinking. "Hey, would you want to come to a party in a couple weeks? It's for my birthday." He says that part like it doesn't matter for some reason. "It's at my place."

I think about it. This was more fun than I ever could've predicted, but will that fun carry over to a party full of his drunk friends? But he's been great today, so I feel reluctant to hurt his feelings. As if the opinion of a lame kid like me would have any effect on him, but still ...

"I know it's weird to go to some strange house full of drunk people you barely know," he says, like he's reading my mind or something. "You could bring friends, or whatever."

It seems highly unlikely that I'll want to go to a popular kid party, but he's being really cool about it, so I say, "Sure, thanks! Send me the details and I'll see if I can make it." I pull out my phone. "Should we, like, get each other's numbers? I don't check my school email much on weekends, so in case anything comes up ..." I suddenly expect this to be where Benji gets weird and draws the line, but he's already pulling his phone out of his pocket.

He unlocks it and hands it to me so I can put my number in, then pockets it again. "I'll text you so you have mine." He opens the door. "Bye!"

I watch him walking to his car for a couple seconds, then close the door, feeling oddly happy. That was the funnest group project meeting I've ever had with someone who wasn't already a friend. Who knew?

My phone dings in my pocket. It's a text from an unknown number and I open it. "Yo this is Dorian," it reads. I see the three dots meaning there's more being written, and another message pops up under that: "Stone cold baller." I roll my eyes and laugh and start back up the stairs, feeling actually motivated to read the graphic novel and maybe even make some more progress on the book itself.

"Chris?" I stop halfway up and turn. It's my mom standing at the foot of the staircase. Her own phone is in her hand, and she looks unhappy. "Honey, I've got some news."

CHAPTER EIGHT: BENJI

I check my phone for the literal hundredth time. I don't even know why it's bothering me that Chris never got back to my jokey texts, or the ones after that telling him the date, time, and address for my party. I mean, Chris Quinn? I should be thankful he didn't seem to notice my messages.

We're at Cherri's house, hanging out in the attic. Her house is bigger than mine—which is pretty huge I guess—but she likes the attic because no one else comes up here except the cleaner, and because the smell of pot smoke doesn't travel down to the rest of the house; when the fan in the ceiling is on, it just pushes the smoke out. It's not attic-y seeming at all up here—there's a comfy sofa, bean bag chairs, moody lighting, and a mini-fridge with sparkling waters and sodas.

We're calling this a study session, which means everyone's got their phones out looking at guys they like while we smoke up and eat snacks and talk shit.

"Do you even *hear* yourself?" Cherri is being Cherri, giving Alicia a withering stare, her hand poised above a tiny dish of soy sauce holding a dripping piece of tuna sashimi in chopsticks.

"Ugh, I know," Alicia sighs. She traces a finger longingly down her phone screen, staring at it, then thrusts it at Cherri and Tiara. "But, like, look at those abs!"

Cherri flicks her gaze across the photo. "Look, fuck him if you want to," she says dismissively. "But, like, the homecoming dance?"

"I'd feel bad just using him for sex." Alicia's already lost this argument and she knows it. "He was just so, I don't know ..." She trails off. "The way he asked me ..."

"He bought you a gas station rose!" Tiara says, every word dragged out in disgust. The others laugh—me included, if I'm honest, though I don't feel good about it. Cherri chimes in again.

"Seriously, where do you think this could go? His dad is a *janitor*. His mom—I don't think she's legal. She barely speaks English and she has that scared look at parents' night things, like she thinks ICE is gonna grab her and deport her." Val starts to protest and Cherri shoots her a look. "I'm not saying that's right or that she's a bad person, okay? All are welcome or whatever. I'm just saying, where's the future in dating Emilio?"

"I wish I had pork rinds," Everly says dreamily, out of nowhere. The room cracks up again. Cherri never has snacks like that—it's always sushi, or caviar, or Brie cheese and fruit salsa with fancy little crackers. "That's it!"

Tiara shouts. "Guys like Emilio are like pork rinds. You might crave them sometimes but you'd never let them in your house."

"I *know*," Alicia says again, sounding defeated.

"Can we go get pork rinds though?" Everly pleads.

"Okay, calm down, girl!" Cherri says. "Val, can you drive?" Val's by far the only one in any shape to drive right now, and her car is her parents' old SUV (old as in five years old), so she's also the only one who can fit all six of us comfortably.

We stop at the gas station (where Tiara, full of hilarity, tries to give Alicia a plastic-wrapped rose down on one knee) for Everly's disgusting snack of choice. Then Tiara wants to drive by Ben's house, and that starts off a whole thing of driving by the houses of crushes. ("Don't even ask," Cherri warns Alicia, as if she'd even mention Emilio's name at this point. "We are *not* going to the ghetto to get carjacked.")

"What about you, Benji?" Val asks, looking at me in the rearview mirror. "Who do you want us to help you stalk?" I feel like she's trying to be nice and make sure I'm included, but I'd rather not.

I think about the one guy's address I do have saved in my maps app. Even if I did like Chris that way, I can't imagine bringing up his name in Cherri's presence. And I *don't*—I couldn't even stand the guy before our meetup, and though I have to admit he's pretty cute when he's not acting all hyper and obnoxious, it's *not* a crush. Plus the way he reacted when I suggested doing the gay diary entries told me everything I need to know about his sexuality.

"I, uh, don't know his address," I settle on as the excuse I hope will get the attention off me.

"You mean Lance?" Everly says. "I know where he lives."

"Uhh ..." I stall. I wasn't thinking of him, obviously, but I don't feel like talking about *why* I don't really like him anymore. Plus, he's a good decoy to distract the girls from learning about anyone I *do* really like. Not that I like anyone in particular at the moment, I tell myself firmly.

Everly takes that for a "yes." "Take the next left," she tells Val.

I'm laughing and joking with everyone, somehow, though I barely know what I'm saying. All I can think about as Everly directs us toward Lance's house is the last time we saw each other.

We'd planned to meet outside the locker room after school for a few minutes, before he had to start hockey practice. It started out pretty great. "Look what I got," he said, holding up a key on a plastic spiral thing. "It's for the sports supply closet. Come on!" He grabbed my hand and pulled me into the locker room and off to the right. I could hear the other guys' voices talking and laughing, and the sound of locker doors clanging, but that was all coming from the opposite direction. I let Lance pull me along, feeling my heart start to pound, until we got to a plain metal door. He slipped the key in and stood aside so I could go in.

It was dark until Lance came in behind me and pulled a string dangling from the ceiling and a dingy bulb came on above us, the light dimmed by a dirty, yellowed plastic shade. He shut the door and locked it behind us and grinned. "I thought we should have a little privacy."

We started kissing, and even though it was exciting to have snuck into this hidden spot, the making out was pretty much like always, with me wondering if he was putting on a show instead of really liking it, and trying not to get in my own head too much about that to the point where *I* stopped enjoying it myself.

But then I started to feel like this time should be different. We'd always made out in out-of-the-way places, like behind the school or in an empty classroom, but always where people could come across us at any time. This was the first time we had a locked door between us and anyone else. Real privacy, like Lance had said. Maybe we should be going a little farther. Maybe Lance was expecting us to, and waiting for me to make the first move.

So I got up my courage. I pulled back from kissing, looked him in the eye in what I hoped was a really intense, sultry way, and slowly knelt down on the closet floor, trailing my hands down his body as I went. I unfastened his belt and fly. It was super weird and kind of exciting and surreal as I reached through the opening on the front of his boxers.

I'd only done something like this once before, over a year ago with a strange guy at a party who I never saw again, but right away I noticed a difference. That guy had ... felt excited by the time we got to this part. Lance didn't, and that should've maybe been a warning to stop, but I figured I could coax him into it. So I put my all into it, trying to get the reaction I was hoping for, and ... nothing. It just stayed the way it was, and nothing I could do could get it to respond.

After a few minutes of pointless effort, I stood up, feeling completely humiliated. Lance fastened his pants back up and tried to salvage the situation with some more making out, but after a minute, I said I had to get going. Before I left he held my chin in his hand and looked into my eyes. "Hey," he said. "That was really cool. I think I just have to pee, that's all." I nodded and smiled and said I understood, and that was that.

That was a few days ago, and I've kind of been avoiding him since then, or at least not seeking him out, and hoping I won't run into him. And now here I am in a car full of my friends, high as hell, driving straight toward his house.

We get there before I can even fully process how wrong and stupid this all feels. But at least we'll just drive slowly by, looking for lights or silhouettes in the bedroom windows, and then take off again. It won't be that bad.

"There he is!" squeals Tiara, and I look out the window, my heart sinking. Lance has apparently just pulled up to his house and is getting out of a car. Only he's getting out of the passenger side. He leans down at the open door like he's talking to the driver, then straightens up and closes the door. The driver does a U-turn and pulls away as we pull up, and I can see it's a girl. I only get a glimpse of long blond hair under a stocking cap, but she looks familiar; I think she's a senior at our school.

"Lance!" Everly calls out the window she's just rolled down, and I wish I could actually shrink into the leather of the second row seat where I'm sandwiched between her and Tiara, but there's nowhere to go, so I try to look unconcerned. Lance hears her and walks over, bends over with his hands in the pockets of his letter jacket.

"Hey Everly," he says with the same dim smile he always seems to have on his face. Then he looks farther in and spots me. I attempt a casual non-humiliated smile; who knows how it comes out? "Hey Benji, how's it going?"

"Oh, you know," I say vaguely. "How about you?"

"Pretty great, I guess." He looks around at the other occupants. "Listen, ladies, you mind if I steal Benji for a second?"

"Not at all," Cherri says from the front seat. I feel like she's either laughing at or pitying me, despite her pretty neutral expression and voice. Thank *fuck* none of them know about the supply closet incident; it's bad enough they just witnessed Lance getting dropped off after what was probably a date with that girl.

Everly opens the door and hops out so I can get out. I move a little slowly, feeling like I'm marching toward my own doom or something. Everly gives me a sympathetic look as I pass her, and then she gets back in and shuts the door, rolling up the window.

Lance peers up at the streetlight we're under and takes my elbow, leading me a little ways down the sidewalk where it's darker and we're not right next to the car full of girls.

"Hey, I wanted to make sure we're okay," he says, looking down at me. He's only a couple inches taller than me but with his muscles it seems like a lot more. Usually I find it sexy, but right now it just makes me feel small and unimportant. "About me going out with Bella. I figure we're not, like, exclusive or anything, right?"

I shake my head.

Lance nods, looking thoughtfully into the distance. "Yeah, I really think my sexuality is, like, pan, you know? Where I can just be with whoever whenever, right?"

That's not what pansexual means! I want to scream in his face, but I just want to get out of this situation with whatever shreds of dignity I have left, so I just mumble "Sure" under my breath. He does that chin-cupping thing again; I guess that's his boss move or something.

"Hey, and like, about the other day," he begins, and I have to really stop myself from groaning out loud. "I'd be totally up for trying that again. I just gotta be in the right headspace, but I think it could be really cool."

I will never ever go down on you again, I think. But I don't even know if I really mean it, so I don't say that either. "Maybe." I try for another matter-of-fact smile.

"Cool," he says, still holding my chin, and gives me this kiss that's trying to be all deep and passionate, but I can barely respond. All I can think about is whether my friends are staring through the windows trying to see what we're doing. My back is to them, but for all I know they're doing just that. Maybe Lance sees that and he's putting on even more of a show for them. God.

"Okay, well …" I pull away as politely as I can. "I gotta go now." Then I make the interminable walk back to the car, trying to look like I don't have a care in the world, when in reality all I want to do is curl up and yell into a pillow for the rest of the night.

CHAPTER NINE: JEMMA

An office aide knocks on the classroom door and brings a slip of paper to my teacher, Mrs. Wolfred. I'm in fourth period, AP History, and we're having a class discussion about the parallels between the Great Depression and what's going on in our economy today. Cheery stuff.

But I'd rather talk about economic problems for another four hours than follow the aide to the main office for a talk with Mr. Stafford, my guidance counselor.

I swear, you get good grades your whole life and it generally keeps the school out of your face—I mean, except for the occasional honor roll announcement or whatever. I've always gotten pretty much straight A's and I'm enrolled in all the advanced placement classes except math and science (no thank you, ugh), and the only time I've had to talk to the guidance counselor was to firmly tell him no, I wasn't interested in going the AP calculus and physics routes and was sticking to the regular math and science classes until I'd fulfilled my requirements for an advanced degree.

But now that it's time for college stuff—SATs and early decision and visits and everything—this is apparently where the rules reverse and it's the *good* students who get all the attention, like it or not. This is about the fifth time I've talked to Mr. Stafford this *semester*, and it's only November. Ugh.

I sail past the secretary, who knows me by sight now, and into his office. He looks up from his computer and gives me a smile that's half friendly, half worried. "Hi Jemma, thanks for coming." (*Like I have a choice?*) "I just wanted to see how it's going with applying.

Early application deadlines are right around the corner for a lot of schools. In fact Bard's has already passed. Did you decide to go for them?"

Shit, right into it with no pleasantries. Things are getting serious, I guess. "No, I decided to pass on early decision. I haven't settled on just one school, so I'm going to apply for regular admission to a few different ones. Bard included." I flash him a bright smile.

He nods, his forehead creased. "Well, luckily that shouldn't cause any problems for *you*, not with your academic record. Now I don't know much about the process of applying to fine arts programs; are you going to submit samples of your art as well as the traditional essay?"

My smile gets wider. "It depends on the college. Each one is a little different, but yeah, some of them will take that."

"What about letters of recommendation? Who are you planning to ask for those? Remember teachers need at least a couple weeks' advance notice because they're doing them for a lot of students."

On and on it goes. I try to put Mr. Stafford at ease with every answer. I just want him off my back; how can anyone concentrate on writing the perfect essay or picking the best pieces of art to represent them with him breathing down your neck like this? But finally he seems satisfied by my answers and lets me go with a promise (threat?) to check in again soon.

Breathing a sigh of relief, I'm so eager to bounce that I almost don't recognize the guy coming from the other wing of the office, the health section. Even if I wasn't in such a hurry I might've missed him, even though I'm really good with faces. He looks even paler than he did that day in the bookstore, and the hood of his sweatshirt is up, covering most of his hair and putting his eyes in shadow.

"Chris?" He turns, slowly, as if my voice only gradually gets through to him. It *is* him, but wow, he looks way different from the smiley, blushing curly-haired kid I teased at the store, gawky and eager like a puppy. His eyes have dark smudges under them and his lips are pressed together and turned down at the edges.

"Hey there!" My voice seems too bright for the mood he's giving off but I can't stop myself. "Did you get your special order?" I know he has, of course, because I've checked the records, but it's the only thing I can think of to say.

"Oh." He looks puzzled for a second, and I feel weirdly mortified by the thought that he doesn't even recognize or remember me. But then his eyes clear a little. "The *Dorian Gray* thing. Yeah, thanks."

"Great." We walk out of the office side by side, and I feel like I've never felt this awkward in my life. I can't wait to get out of this situation. I turn to say goodbye ... and see his face start to crumple like he's going to cry.

"Oh, hey, hey ... Are you okay?"

He nods quickly, but he's clearly not. I check the time; still half an hour left of fourth period, but my teacher probably doesn't expect me to have gotten out of Mr. Stafford's clutches this quickly. And we both have paper passes in our hands, so no one is going to hassle us.

"Come here." I lead him downstairs and into the space under the stairs. It's not like it's totally private if people come by, but at least it's a little out of the way. His shoulders are shaking by the time I get him sat down on the floor against the wall. I sit next to him. "What's going on?"

He takes a shaky breath. "It's my grandpa." His voice rises at the end into a little sob. All awkwardness forgotten, I put my arms around him and pull his head down onto my shoulder. He's so much taller than me that he has to curl into what seems like an uncomfortable position to get there, but he does it, and cries into my sweater.

I rub his back until he calms down enough to talk again, haltingly. I find out that his grandpa's been suffering from Alzheimer's but doing pretty well, until he suddenly went downhill over the course of a couple days. His grandma had been taking care of him at home, but it had gotten so bad so fast that he'd been put in a nursing home in a wing that's basically a hospice for really severe dementia cases.

Chris tells me he'd been in the habit of visiting his grandpa every couple days when he lived at home, and coming over whenever his grandma needed extra help. But he hadn't been to visit either of them since it had happened. He says he keeps making excuses to his family and feeling more and more guilty about abandoning his grandpa. But he's scared of seeing him like that and what it'll feel like. "They all expect me to be the happy funny one," he says. "What if I can't? What if I'm just a basket case, like I'm being now? That'll just make everything worse for everyone."

He keeps saying he's sorry—for crying, for laying his problems on me, for being weird, for getting my sweater wet, for wasting my time— and I keep having to tell him to stop. I barely know the guy, but there's something so vulnerable and helpless about him, all I want to do in this moment is just be there for him.

After he's calmed down, or at least stopped sobbing, we stay the way we are for a while longer. It's nice to feel his body gradually relax against me. It should be weird to be cuddling a random stranger, especially for this extended period of time, but somehow it isn't.

Finally he raises his head and scrubs his face against his sweatshirt and starts to apologize again. "It's fine," I cut him off, and we both laugh a little, but I realize I don't want to send him off into the world again without support. "Let me give you my number, okay? If you need anything, I want you to text me."

He looks surprised, but he doesn't argue. I remember my impression of him back at the bookstore, that he was imprinting on me like a baby chick. Now he really is, I think. And I find myself feeling okay with that.

CHAPTER TEN: CHRIS

I'm sitting in my parked car, wondering what I've gotten myself into, when I see her front door open and close. Jemma runs down the walkway of her house and peeks in to make sure it's me before opening the door and getting in.

"Sorry," she says breathlessly. "I suddenly couldn't find *anything*. I even managed to lose my phone *after* you texted that you were here."

I laugh, trying not to sound tense. This is absolutely not a date, which she made sure to let me know when I asked her. So why do I feel like how I imagine I would if I'd ever been on a date?

"No worries." It's probably better that she took a few extra minutes; I suddenly think that the start time of a party is not the time you should actually show up. I picture us being the first ones there and my stomach seizes up a little.

I had no intention of going to Benji's party; I actually forgot all about it, with the news of my grandpa coming so soon after the invitation. Even when he sent me the details the day after our meetup, it didn't really register. But when Jemma texted me to get my number in her phone, I suddenly saw Benji's messages again. For a couple days after that, I thought about it off and on. Maybe I needed to do something out of my routine to take my mind off things. Benji's party started to seem more and more like the thing that could do that.

And it also felt like something Jemma could help me with—which she seemed to want to do; she'd texted me almost daily since our strange but nice time under the stairs. She's way more popular and confident (like actually confident) than I am, and she's probably been to a hundred high school parties versus my grand total of zero. I finally decided to ask her to go with me.

Almost as soon as I sent the text, I felt stupid. For a couple nerve-wracking hours, she didn't respond, but finally she got back to me. "Yeah I can do that." Pause. "You do remember I'm gay tho, right?" I was never so glad to be texting instead of talking in person, so she couldn't see the purplish red my face probably was, judging from how hot it felt.

"Of course!" I wrote back. "I just don't want to go alone. I think it'll help distract me from stuff."

And here I am, with her sitting next to me, realizing we haven't actually seen each other in person since the day she had me wrapped in her arms for like half an hour.

"So, Benji's birthday party," she says. We hadn't really talked much over the texts except to get her address and figure out a time. "You know him well?"

"No, not really." God, this was probably such a bad idea. "We're working on a project for English together. And, like, everybody knows him, at least juniors do."

"Oh yeah, seniors know him too." Her voice sounds like she's holding something back, and I feel like I need to justify going to his house.

"I never thought about hanging out with him; his friends are, well, *you* know." I start the maps app on my phone and wait for it to give me the first direction. "But he seemed pretty nice when he came over for the assignment. I don't know. I wasn't gonna go, but my head's been a mess. I can't concentrate on anything anyway."

"Totally." She says it kind of reassuringly and I feel less embarrassed, though that only lasts about a second. "Well, I'm happy to be your wingwoman if you're looking to meet girls ... or whoever?" She looks over at me and I'm glad for the darkness.

"I'm not really looking for that." I don't know what else to say; she's the closest thing to a crush I've had in a while, but obviously *that's* not an option, and I can't even imagine flirting with any of the girls that are probably going to be at Benji's party.

She laughs and pokes me in the ribs. "Then we'll just get a little drunk and hang out." I'm relieved that she drops the topic so easily.

We arrive at Benji's house, and it's crazy massive by my standards. We have to pull past it to park on a side street, because the narrow road between his front yard and the lake doesn't allow parking. I suddenly recall him complimenting my house and wonder how he managed to act so nice about it. You could fit my whole house in his living room, I bet.

We walk back after parking and get to the front, and there's a note taped to the door that says DO NOT RING. Oh right. He said that in his texts (also in all caps, I remember now). I pull out my phone and scroll back through the messages to remind myself where we're supposed to go instead. "I guess it's around back."

I lead the way (not very confidently) around the side of the house and across a huge back lawn, worrying that motion sensor lights are going to pin us to the grass like incompetent cat burglars. Then I see lights shining in the windows of what looks like a little house connected to the garage. I head toward it and see a few people hanging around outside it. Although I'm nervous to approach them, at least it seems to be confirmation that this is where the party is.

I recognize a couple members of Cherri's group (and I guess Benji's, although I've kinda come to think of him as separate from the mean girls; which is awfully generous of me based on exactly one interaction with him, but whatever). I don't know their names; they're some of the less vocally mean ones.

"Hey," one of them says neutrally as we walk up.

"Hey," I say back. "Is Benji around?" You probably don't ask for the host when you come to a high school party, I realize, feeling like an idiot.

"Yeah, he's in there," the other one says. Either they don't sense blood or they're feeling merciful; for whatever reason they don't mock me for being such a dork. I head inside with Jemma close behind me.

I don't see Benji, but I do see a kitchen with coolers of drinks on the counter. It's obviously pretty early in the party, but there are a few people standing around and music playing on invisible speakers, so at least it's not like it hasn't started, I think with relief.

I brought a present but don't see anything resembling a gift table. It's a joke gift anyway; I figured I couldn't get a rich kid like him anything he wouldn't already have (only ten times better), but I've literally never gone to someone's birthday party without bringing them *something*. (Although the last time I went to one was way before I hit high school.) I'm really glad the thing I brought is small enough to fit in my jacket pocket so I can just forget I did something so lame in the first place.

Jemma and I dig through a cooler. I grab a light beer and she finds a hard seltzer. I realize she's still wearing her coat. It's not that cold; we probably could've left them in the car but I didn't think of it. I take mine off. "I'll find somewhere for our stuff." She shrugs hers off and hands it to me, and I go off in search of somewhere to stash them.

The little house is surprisingly roomy; I don't see a bedroom at first, but I do notice a narrow set of stairs at the back of a kind of den that has a couch and a big TV. I climb them to find a second floor under the roof, with slanty walls like an attic. There's a big bed and I see a few coats on it. I lay mine and Jemma's on the corner, where I hope I can find them easy if and when we leave early (as I assume we will).

My phone dings and I look at it. It's Marty, asking if we can have a movie night. I swear I told him I'd be out and that he was my cover if my parents asked. It's totally possible he just forgot; for obvious reasons he can be kind of a space cadet. I sit on the edge of the bed and write him back, and before I know it we're deep in a jokey text chain. I only notice how long I've been sitting there when I realize my beer is gone and I, lightweight that I am, have a good healthy buzz on.

CHAPTER ELEVEN: BENJI

I make one run to the main house to make sure my mom's in bed with her TV turned up loud and a glass of wine and that all the doors are locked and blinds and shutters down. Then I head back to my place.

I've had what's called the "carriage house" to myself for a couple years now. When I turned fifteen, my dad had a new kitchen and bathroom installed and made a bunch of other improvements, and I moved in there pretty much full time. I mean, I come back to the main house for some meals and to hang out with my parents sometimes, but I spend a lot of my time in the carriage house.

It's really convenient because I can have friends over and don't have to worry about parental supervision. I still don't like to have people over too often though; even though it's a cool setup for me, it's also kind of weird, and I don't like explaining it or having people comment on it or wanting to see the main house. This whole party thing is making me antsy, but I couldn't find a good way out of it, so here we are. At least no one'll be able to get into the main house, my dad's out of town, and my mom's not gonna notice the commotion happening at my place.

More people have gotten there by the time I get back. It doesn't take many for my little place to not seem empty, but it's also got a surprising amount of room; I know a lot more people are going to be able to fit yet. I see Lance, but he's talking to the girl I saw dropping him off the other night, so I basically run in the opposite direction.

I go to the kitchen for a drink and freeze when I see who's standing by the window. She turns and gives a tense half smile.

"Jemma."

"Hi Benji, happy birthday." She raises her can in a toast.

"What are you doing here?" I realize it sounds ruder than I meant it to. Luckily she doesn't rise to the bait and get angry, at least not visibly.

"I came with someone."

"With ... Monica?" Not that she was invited either, so that wouldn't explain her presence.

"No, just a ... friend." Jemma hesitates. "I mean, Monica's just a friend too, but ..."

"Oh, I didn't know. I'm sorry."

"It's okay. It's better this way."

"Oh, okay." I shift awkwardly. "So how's it, uh, been going otherwise?"

"Pretty good, I guess. Getting ready for college, mostly. Did you hear about the dance the GSA is putting on?"

"Yeah, yeah I did," I say carefully. "How's that going?"

"Great. We've actually sold a lot of tickets. It's looking like it's gonna be pretty big." She hesitates. "Are you coming?"

"I, uh, I don't know. I've got a lot of, you know, things going on."

"Right," Jemma says. "You haven't had time for a GSA meeting in, gosh, over a year, I guess."

"Yeah ..." I trail off.

"Guess Cherri wouldn't approve." Jemma's matter-of-fact tone seems forced.

"What? She's not—"

"Yeah," Jemma cuts me off. "She kind of is. I heard how she's been trash-talking the queer prom to anyone who'll listen."

"But that's not because she's, like, homophobic. She just thinks—"

Jemma interrupts again. "She just thinks anything that's for everyone, that's all inclusive, has to be trash."

"Look, Jemma ..." I try to pick my words carefully. "I'm sorry I stopped coming to the GSA. It's just—well, maybe I don't need it anymore. I know I'm gay and I'm fine with it;

my friends are fine with it too. There's a time to just live your life, you know?"

"Sure, Benji, whatever." It's not exactly pleasant, but at least it seems like a place to end this argument.

"So, uh, who *are* you here with?" I try to sound conversational, not suspicious.

She shrugs. "Just a guy I'm kind of friends with. Chris Quinn? He said you know him from class?"

That's genuinely surprising. He's a junior and she's a senior; she's all involved in everything and he seems like, well, kind of just like he's goofing off. She's gay and he's ... clearly not, as far as I could tell when we hung out. Although now I'm kind of wondering, since most of Jemma's friends are in the GSA (and there's not much non-queer sexuality represented in the Genders and Sexualities Alliance, at least there wasn't back when I was a more active participant).

"Yeah, that's right, we're just doing a thing for school," I say. "Where is he?"

She looks around and shrugs. She starts to say something but her phone buzzes in her jeans. She pulls it out and frowns at the screen. "I'll see you later, okay?" She heads outside, already typing as she goes.

Tiara comes in a minute or two later and gives me a hug, squealing "Happy birthday!" We chat for a little bit and I direct her toward the drinks (and the edibles stashed in a drawer that I figure we'll only hand out little by little so nobody overdoes it and freaks out). I take her coat from her and bring it upstairs to my bedroom.

There's a half-wall thing that separates the room from the stairs. As I climb far enough up to see over it, I spot Chris, sitting among the coats on my bed, grinning to himself and texting someone. He doesn't notice me until I toss Tiara's coat on the bed. He looks up with a little jump and sticks his phone in his back pocket.

"Oh hey, Benji." He stands and starts to raise his arms like he's about to hug me, but he ends up shoving his hands in his pockets instead. "Uh, thanks for inviting me to your party."

"I didn't know you were coming," I say. "You kind of ghosted me after I texted you." Why do I sound weirdly needy about this stupid kid not texting me back? I have no idea.

"Oh, did I?" His eyes seem a bit distant all of a sudden. "Sorry about that. I—I've had a lot going on."

"Are you gonna be able to send me your half of the assignment soon?" Am I literally asking about a school project on the weekend at my birthday party? What the hell is wrong with me?

"Yeah, I will, I promise. It's just been ... kinda rough lately. Sorry."

I laugh it off, because what the fuck am I even saying? "No biggie. I'm glad you could make it after all. Did you get something to drink yet?"

"Yeah." He grabs an empty beer can off my nightstand. "I could use another though." I notice his cheeks are a little flushed, even though his eyes look kind of ... hollow, I guess?

Almost like he's got bruises under them, or dark circles like he hasn't been sleeping well.

"I ran into Jemma," I say. "You brought her, right?"

"Yeah." He smiles a little and I wonder if he's got a crush on her. Poor guy.

"You know her from ... art class?" It's the only possibility I can think of besides the GSA.

He laughs. "No, I can't do art. I'm still at the finger painting level. I was really awesome in pre-K but it's gone downhill from there." He flicks his eyes to the desk near my bed, which has a bulletin board over it with a few illustrations tacked to it. "You're an artist, though, huh?"

I shrug. "I used to be really into drawing comics, but I haven't done it for a while."

He moves closer to the desk and studies my drawings for so long I start to feel self-conscious. There's a small stack of sketch pads on a shelf, and he pulls them down and starts flipping through them. "These are fucking cool!" He sounds like he means it. "You're really really good. You should keep doing it."

I've gotten so used to my friends looking at it as a weird, like, glitch of my personality that I don't even know how to respond. "Thanks?" I change the subject. "So what do *you* do for fun? I mean, outside of school?"

"You mean besides watch old movies with my stoner buddy and my ..." He doesn't finish the sentence, and his eyes get a little distant like they were when I first came in. Then he laughs without sounding amused. "I guess it's kind of predictable, but I've been working on developing a, like, standup comedy routine."

"Really?"

"For real." He shrugs. "I'm hoping to get it ready in time for the talent show. Trying to use my powers for good not evil for a change." We both laugh at that.

"Can you do a little bit for me?" I'm teasing, but his eyes widen like he misses the sarcasm.

"Oh, I, um, don't think I—"

"Relax, I was kidding." I smile, and he does too, with relief. He's actually really cute when he's not making faces and acting up. "What's it about though? The routine you're working on?"

"Oh, the usual standup shit, about how I'm a worthless loser with a pathetic life. It's comedy gold, and it's also easy to come up with; I just look in the mirror and talk about what I see."

That surprises a laugh out of me because he says it in a funny way, but then I feel a little bad. Because while I might not've used those exact words, that's about what I would've said about him if anyone had asked me before we hung out. Plus, even if I were still thinking bitchy things like that about him, it's always hard to hear someone put themselves down. "That's probably not true, but it's really cool that you're gonna be in the talent show."

"Not really." He looks down kind of shyly.

"It is," I say firmly. "You wanna go get another drink?"

"Hell yeah." A big smile reappears on his face.

CHAPTER TWELVE: JEMMA

"Wanna come over?" The text hangs there for a second, and then a follow-up comes fast: "Netflix & chill?" Then a smiley face. "Or at least Netflix & snax?"

It's the first time Monica has willingly interacted with me, other than the bare minimum needed to run the GSA, since I rejected her weeks ago. I'm relieved she reached out; I didn't mean to make things tense between us again.

"Can't." After a pause, I add a smiley emoji too. "I'm at a party."

"Bummer! Can't you leave early?"

"I came with someone." As soon as I type that, I wonder if it came off wrong. I add, "A friend." Then wonder if *that* came off defensive, like I'm hiding something.

A few seconds tick by. I shiver a little, realizing I went outside without my jacket that Chris disappeared with a while ago.

"Who?"

"Just a guy I know. Don't think you know him."

"I can come get you!" She adds a big-eyed emoji to that one.

"I'm not gonna ditch him."

"Heavenly Creatures? Ginger Snaps?" I smile, half annoyed and half charmed. She's tempting me with my favorite thing, creepy lesbian movies.

"Some other time."

"You on a date with him or something?"

I snort. "lol please"

"Wasabi peas & kettle corn?" She piles on more temptations.

"My love language!" She *does* know my very favorite snacks. "But no."

There's a pause. "Not trying to get back together." I stare at the words, wondering if she means it. "We can just have fun."

If only that were true, I think. It's not like I don't find her attractive. Friends with benefits would be great. I'm just afraid I'd get sucked into going out with her again. And having to break up with her again.

"I can't okay? See you Monday." I turn my phone on silent, no vibrate, so I don't have to know whether she writes back or not until later. Then I head back into Benji's place.

He's in a corner with a couple of his rich popular friends. Chris is in the kitchen with another beer. His eyes look bright and his cheeks are flushed, and he gives me a big hug. "Hey, I was wondering where you were!" He must be tipsy because I didn't think we were hugging-level acquaintances—but then again, I basically held him in my arms for like half an hour, so what else *would* it take to get to that level? Anyway, there's something adorable and floppy about him, like an overgrown puppy, so I don't mind.

"Let's explore," he says, and I follow him to the back of the house, where there's a room with a pool table, dart board, and video game setup with a leather couch and big screen TV. This seemingly little place has more room than I realized.

"Choose your weapon!" Chris gestures at the entertainment options. "I warn you, I'm pathetically bad at all of these things, so I won't be a challenge no matter what we play."

"Let's play pool. I'm pretty bad at it too, so you might get lucky."

We set up and start playing, and yeah, we're mostly just knocking the balls around, randomly getting them in the pockets once in a while, laughing at our own incompetence. I think about asking him about his grandpa, but then I remember that this party is to distract him from that, so I let it be. I get another hard seltzer and grab him a third beer—he made it through his second one pretty fast. The room fills up as we're slowly getting through our game, and finally I win, kind of, we think— we're both pretty foggy on the rules—so we surrender the table to another pair who've been watching and waiting for their turn.

"Hey, did you know Benji is an artist?" Chris says.

"Yeah." Even though we never had art classes together, being in different grades, there was a time when Benji and I were pretty close.

"Let's go look at his drawings—he's pretty good!" Before I can answer, Chris bounds out of the room and I follow him, up the stairs to the second level, which is pretty much a giant bedroom with coats thrown all over the bed and floor. Chris leads me to a desk and bulletin board, pointing out his favorite illustrations. I remember Benji's style, line drawings that suggest more than they show. They'd be almost abstract but every pen stroke is intentional, so you know exactly what everything is. Even though I'm annoyed with Benji, I can't help but admire his work.

"I know you're an artist too, but I've never seen what you do," Chris says. "Do you have pictures of it?"

As a matter of fact I do, because I've been photographing pieces, trying to decide what to send to colleges. I pull out my phone, ignoring the little red number showing I have new texts, and go to my photos, flipping through. Chris shoves aside a bunch of coats, making a spot on the bed where we can sit side by side.

"I do kind of Cubist-inspired painting, mostly." I don't see any understanding of that term on his face, but he nods anyway and leans over to see them. I show him a couple of portraits, all women, some of them nudes.

"That's really cool." He points at one. "I love all the colors and shapes." He sits up a little. "I don't know anything about art; sorry if that's a stupid thing to say."

"There's no stupid observations about art, it's whatever moves you about it that's important." He leans back down, his chin slowly settling on my shoulder as I flip through more photos of my paintings. It's weird how physically, like, *familiar* we've gotten. He comments from time to time, and I'm pleased with the details he notices. Even though he's obviously not educated in art history or appreciation, he somehow zeroes in on the parts of my paintings that mean the most to me.

While we've been looking at my phone, his arm's found its way around me, and it doesn't feel like he's making some kind of clumsy move; it's just natural, the way that his appreciation of my art is unforced and honest. His cheek against mine as he rests his head on my shoulder also feels like the most natural thing ever. I turn to look at him, he lifts his head to face me, and for this weird moment that seems to last forever, it's like we're being drawn together, like magnets. We're going to kiss, and it seems so right.

And then I snap back to reality. We're going to *kiss*?! I'm a fucking lesbian. What the hell am I thinking?

I pull away and stand abruptly. He looks up, seeming a little dazed.

"I think I'm going home now," I say. "Are you okay to drive?"

He seems thrown off. "Uh, well, I guess I'd like to stay at the party a little longer?"

"That's fine." I realize that a car ride with him would be super awkward right now anyway. Plus he seems a little drunk and probably shouldn't be driving. "I can get a Lyft or something."

"You sure?" He looks up at me. "I could take you home and come back, no problem."

"No, totally, you have fun, okay?"

"Jemma?" He sounds almost childlike. "Did I do something wrong?"

No, you're straight; you did exactly what you're supposed to. I'm the one who was about to do something fucked-up. I discard that possible answer. "No, Chris, it's cool. I just feel tired all of a sudden. You stay and have a good time. I'll see you later, okay?"

I grab my coat and head out, pulling up my texts. Monica, from a while ago: "Okay no worries. Have a good night!" That was surprisingly non-possessive of her, I think. Maybe she really is capable of being chill. I really hope so; otherwise what I'm about to do is going to make things even worse.

"Changed my mind. Still up for coming to get me?"

I don't even have to wait ten seconds before she responds. "Yes!! Send me the address & I'll be there asap!"

I take a deep breath. I hope I'm not leading her on, but right now I could really use some makeout time with a girl to get rid of (or at least forget about) this weird almost-attraction to Chris.

CHAPTER THIRTEEN: CHRIS

Jemma leaves so suddenly I barely have time to react. I dimly think that normally I'd probably be, like, completely humiliated that a girl was so eager to get away from me, but I've got such a good buzz going that it doesn't even bother me too much. I can't help thinking, though, that we were about to kiss before she jumped up … and imagining what that would've been like.

I head back downstairs, holding onto the railing as I realize I'm much wobblier than I was on the way up. The third beer definitely did its job, but it's gone, so I make my way to the kitchen for another one. The night becomes somewhat of a blur, but a happy one. Benji and I run into each other again. He introduces me to people, and I forget their names almost as soon as he says them, but everyone seems to be in a nice, friendly mood, even some of the girls I classify as "mean girls." I almost tell one of them that I think of them that way, but even in my drunk state, I realize that's probably not a good idea.

I join a crowd of dancers for quite a few songs. Then I wander into the game room and get absolutely murdered at videogames—no matter how many times I play with Marty, I'm unrelentingly crappy at any combat or racing type games, and I hardly ever drink so whatever ability I have is out the window. There's so much laughter and music and friendly people everywhere, and it's so perfect, I just want the night to go on forever, and never have to think about my grandpa or anything else sad or difficult ever again.

I don't know how long the party goes on, but at some point I realize there are fewer people there, and the rooms are getting quieter and more empty as more and more people trickle out. My ears feel fuzzy from the loud talking and music; now that it's all slowing down, it's like there's a ringing sound left over.

Some of my many new friends say goodbye as they head out. I close my eyes and lean my head back against the sofa, still basking in the mindless fun. I feel the cushion next to me sink down and open my eyes to see Benji sitting there.

"Hey."

"Hi!" I want to thank him for giving me this amazing distraction right when I needed it, but instead I just find myself grinning like an idiot.

"Everyone else is gone," Benji says. I sit up abruptly and look around. I didn't notice there's no more talking, and the dance music has been replaced by something softer and slower.

"Oh wow," I say stupidly.

Benji laughs. "It's okay." His expression is so much more relaxed and friendly than when I see him in the halls with his friends. "I just wanted to make sure you're okay to drive home."

"Uh, yeah, totally." I kind of have to be, right? "Yeah, let me just get my, uh, stuff." I jump to my feet, but as soon as I do I realize I'm leaning a little to one side. I take a few wobbly steps.

Then I feel Benji's arm around my shoulder. "You sure about that?"

"Yeah ... maybe I need to, I don't know, sit for a little longer?" I can hear my words are slurred. "Sorry, if you need to go to bed I can see if I can get an Uber."

"It's fine—sit down. I'll get you some water." I collapse onto the couch with relief.

Benji brings me a full glass. I reach for it, grab it clumsily, and immediately spill half of it down my shirt. The cold soaking into my shirt makes me gasp. "Oh shit!" I move my hand to try and wipe it away, forgetting I'm still holding the glass, and some more splashes onto me.

Benji laughs and takes the glass. "Yeah, you won't be driving for a while." He holds the water up to my mouth and I kind of slurp clumsily at it, dribbling some more down my chin. That makes him laugh even harder. "We'll try the water thing a little later." He puts the glass down, well out of my reach, and goes to the kitchen. He comes back with a towel and gently presses it against my shirt, soaking up icy cold liquid. My shirt is still damp but at least I don't feel like I'm dripping wet.

"You should try lying down." Benji helps me lean my head against one arm of the loveseat and stretch my legs out over the other arm. He refolds the towel and keeps dabbing at my shirt, his hair falling in his eyes as he works. I feel a fresh wave of affection for him and the night in general.

"You're so cute." I don't know I'm going to say it until I blurt it out, but I know as soon as I say it that I mean it. I've never told another guy that—or even really thought it about one—but it doesn't feel weird at all for some reason. I reach up and stroke his hair back from his face. My fingers feel thick and numb, like they're shot full of Novocain, but revealing his face gives me a little thrill.

"Yeah?" He's kind of smiling like it's a joke.

"No," I say earnestly, working to pronounce words clearly. "You're not just cute. You're like, really really hot." I can hear my R's slurring into sounding kind of like L's and I can tell from his face he's not taking me seriously. I put my hands on his cheeks and stare into his eyes. "I mean it." I'm desperate to be believed for some reason.

Then the room starts to spin a little. "Oh …" I sit up, hoping that'll fix it, but everything I look at seems to be moving. I forget about anything except not getting sick. "I think I need some fresh air."

Benji doesn't hesitate. He helps me up and we go outside. At first the cold feels amazing, but then I start to shiver, and I get worried that the violent shakes will make me more nauseous. "Too cold," I say helplessly.

"You want to go back inside?" When I shake my head, Benji disappears for a minute and comes back with a blanket, which he drapes over my shoulders. That's perfect because I can slip out of it whenever I need more cold, then pull it back around me when I start to shiver too much.

Benji stays by my side, barely saying anything. We walk when I need to move, sit on the dry dead grass when I need to feel anchored to the earth. I fix my eyes on the fence, on the lights from the main house, on the tree branches against the moonlit sky, switching to the next focus point when the moving and shifting of one starts to make me feel like I might throw up. Gradually they start to move a little less. "I need to lay down but stay out here," I tell Benji, hoping he'll help me figure that out. My voice still sounds slurred and distant, but maybe not as bad as before.

He helps me lie on my side, sits next to me, and lets me rest my cheek on his thigh. He brushes my hair back from my forehead, lightly presses his cold palm against my other cheek, and then stops touching me and just lets me lie there, which is perfect.

I start to drift in and out, and thankfully I can close my eyes without feeling like I'm on a rollercoaster now. At some point I feel him help me to my feet. I stumble with every step but he holds me up and slowly guides me inside to a couch. I pour my gratitude at him, though I don't think I move or say a word so I don't know if he feels it. The last thing I remember before passing out is Benji taking my shoes off and covering me with the blanket, tucking the edge under my chin.

CHAPTER FOURTEEN: BENJI

My first thought on waking up is that my hangover isn't bad at all. I think I was too busy playing host to actually drink that much myself.

My second thought is a flashback to Chris stroking my hair and looking at me with a weirdly intense expression. A jolt of adrenaline goes through me and I sit up suddenly in bed. I don't know what the hell that was, but now the dude is passed out in my living room—unless he snuck out sometime in the night. That might be better, I think.

I head downstairs for the bathroom and nope, he's there, still unconscious on the couch. He's curled up so his feet don't stick over the edge anymore and he's snoring lightly.

It's only about nine thirty in the morning on a Sunday—I'm not even sure why *I'm* awake—so I let him sleep while I shower and get dressed. But he's still asleep when I come out of the bathroom, and his phone, lying on the floor, buzzes occasionally, so I finally have to deal with it.

I shake his shoulder gently until he stops snoring and starts to move around like he's waking up. His eyes open, squinting against the daylight coming in through the windows, and then blink and widen, looking genuinely surprised to see me leaning over him. For a second he smiles like he's just blissfully content, but then he starts to get more conscious (and self-conscious). He sits up, scrubbing at his eyes with the heel of his hand.

"Hi," I say. "How ya feeling?"

"Like shit, but better." His voice sounds hoarse. He sees the glass of water from last night and takes a quick gulp. "Sorry about last night. I hope I didn't do anything stupid." He laughs. "I mean stupider than usual."

I think about what he said to me right before he got the spins and wonder if he remembers saying it, but I just laugh with him and shake my head. "You were fine. Glad I could help you not puke. Mostly so I don't have to clean up puke today." I pick up his phone and hand it to him. "It's been kind of blowing up."

His eyes get wide again. "Shit shit shit." He thumbs frantically over to his texts. He reads them and sighs with relief. "My mom's just asking if I fell asleep at Marty's again, and Marty's telling me she's been texting him too." He taps back a couple quick messages and sighs again. "It's all good."

"Well, you can get cleaned up before you go home if you want."

He nods. "I'd take a spare toothbrush if you've got one. My mouth tastes like death." We laugh.

"I've got that, and also some Alka Seltzer. It's a miracle cure." I get him sorted out with a toothbrush in the bathroom and drop two tablets in a little glass of water as he comes out. "Just chug it fast, it's kind of nasty."

"Thanks." he gulps it down, making a face. "I'm really sorry about all this." His face brightens. "Hey, now that my mom thinks I'm hanging out at Marty's, I don't have to rush. Can I buy you some breakfast or coffee or something?"

As if on cue, my stomach rumbles a little. "Well okay, but only if it's hash browns and shitty coffee."

We leave the house, littered with cans and paper plates I'll have to deal with later, and walk around the block to where Chris is parked.

At the drive-through he gets four hash brown patties and two coffees. He hands me half the order and wolfs down one of the patties in a single bite, groaning about how it's burning his mouth. I suggest we take the rest to a lake and give him directions to the nearest one. (There are about five lakes in this part of town.) There's a chilly breeze and the sky is cloudy, but we take our fast-cooling breakfast and walk the asphalt path that leads around the lake.

"Feeling better now?" I say, after what feels like too long of a silence.

"Yeah." He smiles, looking embarrassed again. "I bet you didn't plan on babysitting me when you invited me to your party, huh?"

I laugh. "I don't mind, really." I actually mean it too. It's like night and day, the way he is now compared with how he always acts in class. Plus, having to deal with him was a good excuse to shoo Lance out at the end of the night when he started acting flirty with me (after the girl he'd been flirting with left with her friends).

"I really didn't do anything stupid?" Chris looks hopeful.

"Well ... you did give me a little preview of your standup routine." I manage to keep a straight face until I see his look of horror, and then I burst out laughing. He joins me a second later.

"Shit, you scared me!"

I sip my coffee, hesitating over what I'm tempted to say. Then I go for it. "You did tell me I was hot, though."

"I ... did?" He studies my expression until he realizes I'm not teasing, then turns bright red and looks away so I can't see his face. I wish I could tell if he's disgusted or humiliated or what.

I nudge him with my elbow. "I was flattered." He glances over at me with a guarded expression, probably trying to see if I'm making fun of him again, but then he relaxes a little. He gulps down the rest of his coffee and jogs over to a trash can to throw his cup and hashbrown wrapper away; I follow and do the same.

Chris sticks his hands in his jacket pockets, hunching his shoulders against the breeze ... and then stops for a second. He laughs, pulling something out of his right pocket. It's a little bundle, messily wrapped in the kind of tissue paper you stuff in gift bags, held together with scotch tape.

"I guess since I've already acted like a dumbass I might as well keep it up." He thrusts the package toward me. "I got you a birthday present."

"Oh wow." None of my friends got me presents, and I just asked my parents for gift cards to get music and clothes.

"It's really stupid." Chris sounds apologetic. "I wasn't sure I was coming to your party until kind of last minute, so I didn't have time to get you something good."

I pull at the tape. The tissue paper tears easily and something falls into my hand. It's a heart-shaped locket on a chain, the heart oversized, the fake gold coating cheap-looking like it came from a kid's costume jewelry kit. I turn it over, puzzled. "I found that in my sister's old toys." Chris laughs, embarrassed. "Open it."

I pry the locket open and there are two black-and-white copies of drawings, one stuck in each side. One is a guy in a high collar and tie with a goatee, the other a lady with curly hair pulled up under a hat with big feathers. It takes me a second, but then I recognize them. They're photocopied from the graphic novel version of *The Picture of Dorian Gray*.

"Lord Henry and Sybil!"

"Yeah!" Chris looks relieved that I know what it is. "Since you're being Dorian for our assignment, I thought you might like a souvenir of your two love interests."

I can't stop smiling. It's such a weird, sweet gesture. I can't believe he took the time to put this together. "I shall treasure it always," I say in my best English accent, which is terrible. I hand it to him. "Can you put it on me?"

I turn away and he puts the necklace around my neck, fastening it at the nape. We're both giggling a little at the stupidity of it, but I also can't help feeling a little shiver every time his hand accidentally brushes my skin while he's putting it on. "There," he says, and pats my shoulder.

I turn to face him and hug him without thinking. After a pause he puts his arms around me too. He's a little taller than me and his arms are skinny but strong as they wrap me up. The hug lasts a few seconds past the point of casual. Chris pulls back a little but he's still holding my waist, and our eyes meet and hold each other's gaze. Before I know what I'm doing, I tilt my head up and kiss his lips.

His body stiffens a little like he's caught off guard, but only for a second, and then his lips are responding. My heart is pounding like crazy, and I think for a second that I never had this reaction with Lance, not even once, before I forget to think about anything and just lose myself in the kiss.

"Get a room!" We break apart suddenly as an irritated-looking woman jogs past, panting.

Chris covers his mouth. "Whoops!" he whispers. He looks around as if just realizing that it's mid-morning and we're in the middle of a public place. It's cold enough that the lake isn't crowded, but there are some hardcore joggers and cyclists circling it, and people walking their dogs.

"Sorry. That just ... happened." I'm glad my cheeks were probably already red from the cold. "Um, thanks for the birthday present?"

Chris looks away shyly, but he seems like he's almost smiling. Is he happy or just freaked out?

I realize we're at about the halfway point of circling the lake, so it's going to be a few minutes before we get back to his car whichever way we walk. I start going in the same direction we were before, walking pretty fast. After a minute, Chris catches up to me. To my astonishment, I feel his long, cold fingers touch my hand and then link with mine.

I don't look over and I don't feel like he's looking at me either. We just walk the rest of the way around the lake in silence, holding hands, my mind and my heart racing at this very chaotic turn of events.

Back at his car, he turns on the radio, loud enough that it doesn't feel awkward that we're not talking. He also turns up the heater full blast, though it only really starts feeling warm right as he pulls up to my house. There's no shoulder to stop on, but no one is behind us on the road, so he puts the car in park. "Um." He taps the steering wheel. "Thanks again for taking care of me and not minding that I'm an idiot."

"Oh, that's okay." I touch my chest where the cheap locket is hidden under my coat. "Thanks again for the present."

"It's really stupid." But his smile is different when he says it this time.

"Yeah, I know." I smile back at him. "But it's great."

Chris looks around, then back at me. With a kind of serious look on his face, he leans toward me, and before I know it we're kissing again.

"Well, happy birthday," he says when we stop. I feel like we're both grinning at the weirdness of whatever this is.

"See you later." It's such a strangely normal thing to say when this whole morning has felt so surreal. I jump out of the car and hurry around the side of the house toward my place. I run upstairs and flop on my bed, staring at

the ceiling, wondering what the hell just
happened.

CHAPTER FIFTEEN: JEMMA

Things have gone swimmingly with Operation Re-Lesbify for about three days. Then Tuesday afternoon happens.

Saturday when Monica picked me up from Benji's party, everything went according to my hopes. She took me back to her place, we watched movies about murderous teen lesbians, we ate my favorite snacks, we made out without going too far. No relationship talk either, and no talk about taking out-of-town trips together. We made it through the whole night without it getting weird, Monica dropping me off at home around midnight, and when we texted on Sunday, it was just friendly stuff and plans for the queer prom. Monday and Tuesday during the day when we saw each other in class and in the halls, Monica didn't get clingy or weird.

When we meet in the English classroom after school, she seems happier than she's been since the awkwardness at my place, but she isn't trying to act like we're together again. I'm riding high, a little smug even. Friends With Benefits achievement unlocked! I can have fun with a cute girl from time to time and it doesn't have to become glaringly obvious that, outside of our physical attraction and the activities we have in common, our personalities just don't go that well together.

It's our last day of school before the Thanksgiving break. We're sitting close together with my laptop on the desk between us as I work on the design for a flyer Monica wrote about an activity we came up with to promote the prom before winter break starts. Buy two tickets, give us the name of the person you want to take, and someone from the GSA will go to one of their classes, recite a sonnet on bended knee, and hand them a hand-crafted calligraphy invitation from you. Some of our members are in drama club and had a good fundraiser like that the year before, timed around Valentine's Day, so they came up with the idea (and volunteered to perform the sonnet-o-grams).

We're going to launch it Monday and pretty much run it for the two weeks or so before winter break. I think it's brilliant. Yes it might cause some drama between people, but drama gets attention (and hopefully sells even more prom tickets).

Our backs are to the door, and I don't bother to turn around when I hear Brianna, a sophomore, greet someone coming in. Not until I hear the reply. "Hey, is this the GSA?" I recognize the voice right away. *What the hell*? I have time to think as I look over toward the door of the classroom.

The newcomer catches sight of me and waves, grinning a lopsided smile I know all too well. "Chris?" I ask incredulously. "What are you doing here?"

He crosses the room to where Monica and I are sitting. "Hey Jemma, I just came to see if I could help out with anything. You know, with the dance or whatever."

About a hundred thoughts come through my mind all at once, but the main one is *What's his game?* Why would this straight kid I barely know—except for some weirdly intimate moments we've shared—show up to help plan a queer prom? Does he have a crush on me and hope that somehow this will help him get somewhere? Is he actually gay and I just completely misread what happened Saturday night?

"Welcome!" Monica is blissfully unaware that he's the guy I was with at the party (I stayed vague about the details when she picked me up and she didn't press it). She and Chris introduce themselves to each other and chat for a little bit while my mind races.

I find a place in the conversation where I can break in without seeming rude. "Actually, yeah, could you come with me? We need to get more paper for the printer so we can get these flyers printed."

"Sure!" I jump to my feet and we head out the classroom door. Behind us I hear Brianna call out, "I think we have plenty of paper ..." But I keep going and Chris follows my lead.

We walk down the hall a ways and then I stop. "Hey, can I just ask? Why are you really here?"

Chris's smile falters. "Wh-what do you mean?"

I guess that came out harsh. Not at all how I'm supposed to approach new members. "I mean, you're welcome in the GSA—everyone is—I'm just curious why you decided to come." I try to soften my tone even more. "If you feel comfortable sharing."

"Oh, well, um ..." He pauses and I can't tell if he's trying to find words or making up a story in his mind. "You've been so great about helping me out, I thought maybe this would be a good way to pay you back." He shifts his feet a little and stares down at them. "And, I guess, it'd be good to, like, learn about ... LGBTQ stuff?"

I don't know what to make of that last part at all. Does he mean he's questioning things about himself? Does he want to learn more about it so he can be better friends with me? Or is it something else, like general curiosity?

"Okay, cool." I act like I understand. "Sorry, I didn't mean to come off weird, I was just wondering."

"No worries." Chris smiles again, looking relieved that I backed off my original tone.

I start down the hall again so we can grab a ream of paper from the faculty copier room; I don't want it to be totally obvious that the reason I said I was dragging Chris out of the meeting was just a pretense. While we're walking, I get an idea that might help me suss out what's really going on with him.

"Hey," I say casually. "I'm going to a thing next Monday. It's an all-ages night at this gay club in downtown. You wanna come hang out with me? I don't think anyone in the GSA can make it."

Actually, I just didn't mention it to the rest of the GSA because I wanted a chance to scope out a crowd of queer kids without Monica there. Just in case I get an opportunity to flirt or talk to another girl, I don't want to do it right under Monica's nose. But now I'm more interested in figuring out Chris's deal than I am in trying to score.

"Um, sure ..." Chris sounds hesitant.

"If that's, like, too much queer to take in all at once, that's okay too," I tease.

He laughs. "No, that sounds ... great."

"Great! If you drive to my place, we can take the bus downtown from there."

We head back to the GSA room with a ream of paper, which I put on top of the full ream that was already sitting next to the copier. Brianna grabs Chris to help with some posters. Monica looks at me a little strangely when I sit back down next to her, but she doesn't say anything, and I get back to work on the flyer.

CHAPTER SIXTEEN: CHRIS

A few days after my first GSA meeting, I'm sitting around with Marty in his basement, trying to distract myself from being nervous about hanging out with Jemma later that night. Marty can be a little oblivious, but even he can tell something's up, and so I take a deep breath and spill everything that's happened over the past few days. My not-quite-date and almost-maybe-kiss with Jemma at Benji's party, and then … everything that happened after she left.

I'm blushing furiously as I skim over the details of telling Benji he's hot, and the next day, the weird but amazing time I had with him walking around the lake. I'm pretty confident Marty won't be judgy about me kissing another guy but I wonder if it'll make him uncomfortable. I'm super relieved when he takes it all in like it's no big deal.

I don't really go into how it felt; how exciting and scary it was to take Benji's hand as we walked around the lake, and to go in for another kiss when I dropped him off. I can't really compare it to how I might feel about kissing a girl because I literally haven't kissed any since poor Harriet and I awkwardly made out (if you could even call our smashing together of lips "making out") once during our "going with" phase in middle school. Kissing Benji was way different, and way better.

I've never liked a guy before this, so it's crazy to me that my first real kiss came along with this out-of-nowhere attraction. I've relived all the moments in my mind a hundred times since then, my stomach feeling hollow and almost achy with a bunch of feelings I can't even put words to.

It was so life-changing that it made me think maybe I wasn't really attracted to Jemma. I actually did think that going to the GSA and being around queer kids (besides Benji) would help me sort out my feelings and figure out if I'm actually gay or something.

But as soon as I saw Jemma in the classroom, my world shifted again. Her delicate little body, her mass of blue-streaked black curls, her bow-shaped lips ... I flashed back to sitting next to her on Benji's bed (god this is all so weird) in that moment when I thought we were going to kiss, and I realized that no, I really am attracted to her. And possibly him too. What the hell is wrong with me?

I give Marty the condensed version of all of this. He doesn't have any advice but he's a sympathetic ear at least, and the only person I could ever tell about all this weirdness. And now I'm going on another not-date with Jemma, to a gay club this time. Everything is so backwards about this whole situation. The only good thing about it is that I'm so distracted, I haven't been thinking too much about Grandpa (who I still haven't managed to bring myself to visit in his new "home").

I leave Marty's when it's time to meet Jemma. I hope I can get rid of my jitters before I get to her place, but no such luck; my insides are all tangled up. I ring the bell with her number on it and she comes to the door. It feels like we should be on hugging terms, but instead I give her an awkward wave and smile.

"We've got twenty minutes and the bus stop's really close, so why don't you come up for a few minutes?" I follow her to her place, and she disappears into the bathroom to finish getting ready while I look around. It's small but everything looks amazing, with art up on all the walls and funky mismatched furniture in the living room area. How can my parents' furniture look like an oddball collection of junk, while this equally old-looking stuff looks artsy and cool and goes together perfectly somehow?

When the bus comes, Jemma shows me where to put my money—it's my first time using the city bus—and we're on our way downtown. It's early but already dark, and the streets of Minneapolis are lined with neon lights blinking the names of theaters and bars. There aren't a ton of people out since it's a weeknight, but it's still exciting seeing the city at night, which I hardly ever get to do.

Jemma pulls a cord that runs along the top of the window. We get off the bus and she leads me down a street; I follow blindly, not really knowing the layout of the city or where this club is at all. What little conversation we had on the bus was kind of awkward, but at least now we're moving so it's not quite as weird that we're not talking much.

The club is newish, Jemma tells me, and kind of a speakeasy, so there's no obvious sign outside. She leads me through a plain-looking door and lobby and we take stairs down to the basement level. I can hear thumping music even before we round a corner in a plain concrete hallway and see a guy standing at a little podium outside a door that's got a sign taped to it with the name of the club: Crush.

"Ten dollars each." The guy sounds a little bored. He's dressed in tight pants, platform shoes and a black lacy shirt; I'm sure he'd much rather be in the club than in this dull hallway.

"I got this," I tell Jemma. I pull out a twenty before she can argue and thrust it at the guy, who has us pull up the sleeves on our right arms so he can put a wristband on each of us. He looks up at me with a little smile.

"You've got big hands."

I have no idea what to make of that. "Thanks?" I think I hear Jemma snicker behind me and my face turns red. I suddenly have this terrified feeling like I have no idea what I'm doing, and all my vague visions of something happening with Benji again are just pipe dreams, because why would he bother with a guy who doesn't even know anything about being gay? And how is Jemma going to have a good time tonight with a clueless dork like me tagging along?

The guy opens the door and the music blasts out at us; Jemma goes in first and I follow, trying not to stare at anyone, trying to figure out what to do with my hands. My freakishly big hands, apparently.

There's a coat rack along the wall and we drop off our jackets. "I'll get your drink since you paid for me," Jemma says, and I don't feel like I can argue. "What do you want? There's no alcohol, obviously."

"I'd take a Coke, thanks."

She gets our drinks and we sit on a bench along the wall near the dance floor. It's still pretty dead but people are trickling in. I'm glad she doesn't suggest dancing. I'm feeling awkward enough without worrying about not looking lame on the dance floor.

Our first attempts at conversation are big fails. She asks about my grandpa, which is the last thing I want to talk about. This past Thursday was our first Thanksgiving dinner without him; Grandma came over for a little bit but was obviously distracted and left early to spend some time with Grandpa in his nursing home.

To change the subject, I ask Jemma about college plans, but she seems equally as unenthused to talk about that as I was about my family. I'm thinking her whole idea of inviting me out is a huge mistake and I'm sure she feels the same.

But gradually we get to talking about other things. I start telling her about my plans for the talent show next semester. She's really encouraging, and things start to feel more natural. We talk about the queer prom. Jemma explains more about it, how she hopes it'll be popular enough that maybe students who are exploring their gender or sexuality can kind of act like they're playing along but also get to try out being in an LGBTQ-friendly environment.

"That's really cool. It's probably really scary to think about coming out and having people look at you different."

She nodded. "It should be easier in high school but for some kids, it's even harder, because they've been hiding something for a long time or maybe not even realizing it about themselves until recently, and it's like their public identity feels set in stone to them."

I get that. I sometimes feel like I'm acting up in school because it's what people expect and I don't know any other way to act, and I'm not sure people would see me trying to change, or if they've got such a fixed picture of me that nothing would convince them I'm not just a joke.

But Benji and Jemma both seem to see me differently, and somehow I don't feel the need to be such a spaz around them. Maybe that's why I feel so drawn to them. They give me a chance to be a different version of me that feels new but maybe natural.

"What about you? When did you, like, realize you were—" I realize I don't know what she calls herself.

"Lesbian?" she finishes for me. "I've known since sixth grade. I got a giant crush on a girl I saw in the school play. I never did tell her or anything—we didn't even know each other; she was in eighth grade and had a boyfriend— but I'd daydream about kissing her like all the time. I freaked out whenever I saw her in the halls, got really clumsy and nervous." She laughed. "It was a very nerve-wracking school year, and when it ended, I moped around all summer painting my feelings about how I'd never see her again because she was going to high school the next year. But then in seventh grade, I met a girl who was actually gay too, and we kind of went out."

"So you never really questioned your sexuality." I marvel at that. "You always just knew."

"Yeah, kind of, I guess." She doesn't sound totally sure of that, for some reason. I wonder if she's questioned it since then. But if so, she must've figured it out for sure, because why else would she call herself a lesbian?

"You're going out with Monica now, right?" It seemed pretty obvious when I saw them at the GSA meeting.

"Not ... really." She still sounds hesitant. "I mean, we did ... we were ... but now I'm trying to just be friends with her."

"Are you interested in someone else?" I bite my lip, wondering if that was way too nosy.

"I don't know." The offhand way she says it seems to mean "maybe." She throws my question back at me. "How about you?"

"I don't know," I echo. The words seem to hang between us for a weird little moment, where we're kind of studying each other's faces looking for a clue as to what we really mean by that. At least that's what I'm doing and I imagine she's wondering the same thing.

Jemma excuses herself to go to the bathroom, and I watch the people on the dance floor for a minute. Then my phone vibrates in my pocket.

It's Benji. My stomach flips nervously as I open the text. "Whatcha doing tonight?"

I laugh and look around. "I'm at a gay club actually"

The dots of him replying appear and disappear a couple times as if he's deciding what to write. A message finally pops up. "TBH I didn't know you were gay"

Another one comes quick: "I mean until after my party"

It's my turn to hesitate over what to say. "I'm not sure what I am TBH," I finally type. I wish I could take it back, because now I'm afraid he'll think I didn't like what happened, but I feel too self-conscious to say I *did* like what happened.

He doesn't respond, and I think of and discard a dozen stupid things to write. I look up from my phone, and Jemma is coming across the floor toward me. "Come on, I love this song!" She grabs my free hand. I don't really want to dance, but I don't want to pull my hand out of hers either. So I put my phone back in my pocket and let her tug me onto the dance floor.

Luckily it's a really fast song, so just jumping around seems to be an acceptable dance move judging from some of the other people on the floor. We bounce around, Jemma smiling up at me. It's so fun that I get carried away and scoop her up with my arms around her waist, spinning around in a circle. When I put her down she doesn't immediately move away. The music transitions into a slower, R&B kind of song, and we're kind of moving together, almost but not quite touching, looking each other in the eyes.

Then she breaks the spell, backing away with an expression I can't read, and heads back toward our bench. There's an awkward silence once we sit down. Jemma's examining me like a germ in a petri dish.

"Chris, can I just ask, are you gay?"

I wasn't expecting that at all. I feel my face get hot, hoping the room is too dark for her to see how red my cheeks probably are. "I ... I don't ... think so." She nods and doesn't say anything, like she's waiting for me to explain. "I mean ..." I wasn't ready to say this to anyone, not even Benji obviously, but here it comes. "I ... think I might like guys a little, but I definitely know I like girls." I look down, hoping it's not too obvious I mean her when I say "girls."

She touches my knee lightly, and I jump a little. "Let's go for a walk."

We get our coats, leave the club, and take the stairs to the building lobby. Outside it's cold and crisp, but there's no wind, so walking around isn't too bad. Plus it was getting hot and stuffy in the club, so this is actually refreshing.

"The city looks so magic at night." That sounds so dumb, but I had to break the silence somehow.

"It does." Jemma shivers a little; her coat looks thinner than mine. I put my arm around her shoulders for warmth, and she leans into me a little. We walk to the sidewalk on the edge of a bridge that goes over the river, leaning against the railing to look out at the water.

"It's weird what you said." I think back over our conversation, trying to figure out what she means. "About definitely liking girls but maybe liking guys too." She laughs, but not like she actually finds anything funny. "I always thought I was a lesbian, but recently I've been wondering the same thing." Our eyes meet. "Don't tell anyone I said that, okay? It's like the other thing you said back there, it's scary to think about changing this fixed image of yourself."

"I won't." I glance away. "Don't tell anyone what I said either, okay?"

"Okay." She hesitates. "Chris?"

"Yeah?"

"Can I try kissing you?"

My whole body feels like it's floating, like I'm in a dream. "Okay," I say faintly, not quite believing what she just asked me.

Jemma stands on tiptoes, cups my cheek in her right hand, and very slowly touches her lips to mine, lightly at first, and then leans into it, kissing me more deeply. The city disappears and I pull her close to me.

Afterwards, we take the bus back to her place, sitting side by side. I want to hold her hand but I don't have the courage. But it feels like there's electricity between us, especially where our legs are almost touching.

She walks me to my car and we stand by the driver's side. "I'm not sure what this means."

I laugh a little. "Me either." I think about telling her about Benji—another situation I'm completely confused about—but I'm not sure how. And I don't think *he'd* appreciate me saying anything about what happened between us either. It's just a guess, but he *is* still one of the mean girls, even if he's acted nice to me a couple times. And I'm just a nobody ... who now happens to have kissed two of the coolest people I've ever met, somehow. Disbelief washes over me all over again—and a growing guilty feeling. Does what I just did count as cheating or leading people on? Or do people just kiss each other all the time and it's no big deal? I literally have no idea.

Jemma breaks into my thoughts and it's like she's answering my unspoken question. "Let's just ... keep it between us for now, okay?"

"Sure." I feel less guilty; it doesn't sound like she exactly thinks us kissing meant we're going out or anything, or like she's even sure she's not a lesbian. If she wants to keep her experimenting with a guy a secret from others,

I guess it's okay if I feel the same about what I'm going through, right?

CHAPTER SEVENTEEN: BENJI

Do not, I tell myself sternly for the dozenth time. *Do not waste your energy lusting after another straight boy.*

I'm waiting for Chris to come over for another session of work on the English project. Both of us admitted over email that we've been procrastinating—why Mrs. Frenzi set such a far out due date I have no idea, but now we're almost out of time—so we figure getting together is the best way to force us to make progress on it.

Ever since I got the weird mixed messages from his texts the other night—the surge of hope when he said he was at a gay club and then the total let-down when he said he wasn't sure what he was—I've been practicing tough love on myself, trying not to think anything of the amazing time we had the morning after my party.

Besides, I tell myself, what was I actually thinking, starting to crush on Chris fucking Quinn? I can just imagine how Cherri and Tiara would react if they knew. Big yikes.

This'll be good, I even manage to convince myself. Have him over, prove that when he's not all dazed and hung over, and I haven't just received the silliest sweetest gift ever, we don't have any attraction to each other.

There's a knock on the door and I open it to Chris, looking nervous. As I let him in I notice he's freshly shaved, judging from a tiny cut on his neck, just under his chin. He smells of soap and just a touch too much cologne, and he's wearing a nice gray sweater and dark wash jeans. He avoids my eyes as he says hello, and he doesn't seem to know where or how to stand.

I can immediately tell my side of the bargain of not being attracted to him is out the window. Maybe there's some hope on his side, but then why's he dressed nicer than he was when I saw him at school earlier?

I get sodas and snacks and we sit on the living room couch together, laptops open. We've already got a start on the bio and the essay, so we finish those together. The only thing left is the diary entries.

"I don't know where to start." Chris frowns at an empty page on his screen. "So I'm Lord Henry and I basically want to corrupt Dorian because I'm in love with him and I can't have him?"

"Exactly." I cynically wonder if we should be switching the roles we're playing in this project. "You have to pretend that you're really attracted to a guy, and you don't know what to do about it. Then just write how you're feeling."

He glances over at me, and I see him getting red. He looks away and presses his lips together. Then he starts typing. I lean in to see, and he hesitates, then keeps going.

He's so beautiful, but he's just out of reach. Like he's right there, but I can't touch him, or tell him how I feel. It's driving me crazy.

He looks over and laughs nervously, blushing even harder. "It's so lame, I'm sorry."

My heart is pounding like crazy. "It's perfect." I take a deep breath and touch his leg softly to see how he'll react. He looks at my hand but doesn't move away. Slowly he puts his hand on top of mine. Our fingers link together. This time when we kiss, there's no hesitation from him.

I close my laptop with my free hand and set it on the coffee table. "Guess we made some good progress?" I lean over and take his computer from him, setting it on top of mine.

"Yeah, I can fill in the evil psycho Lord Henry-ness later." He still looks nervous but he's smiling a little. "What about your part, though? Will you be able to, like, channel Dorian?"

"Yeah, it's like a classic love triangle for him in the beginning, right? He loves Sybil but he's, like, under Henry's spell, and he doesn't know which way to go. That's the part I'll write about. Maximum relationship drama!" I grin but Chris's half-smile falters. "You don't think that's a good idea?"

"What?" he sounds dazed for some reason. "No! I mean yeah, I think that's great. Classic."

"Good, then I'll finish it up tonight and we can turn everything in tomorrow." I stroke his hand. "When do you need to get home?"

He bites his lip. "Well, I'm supposed to—I was going to visit my grandpa today, but ... I don't really feel like it." He brightens. "I'll do that another day. Homework comes first, right?"

"Yeah, homework." I smirk and touch his cheek, then lean in for another kiss, and I keep kissing him until he seems to forget whatever's bothering him. At least whatever it is doesn't seem to be any doubt about whether he wants to be making out with me.

After he leaves an hour or so later (with no more homework progress made, unless our kissing and groping could be considered research), I rush through the assignment just to get it out of the way. I find myself looking at the school calendar online for the date of the queer prom. Ugh. Am I really thinking about what I think I'm thinking about?

I finally admit to myself I really really like Chris (and it's crazy but I'm feeling the same intensity coming from him). But then I think about having to deal with the fallout if my friends find out. Maybe that's why it was so easy to write Dorian's diary entries. Feeling pulled two different ways, not sure that happiness lies in either direction. Super relatable.

I start a group text to kind of open the subject of the dance. Then I think twice about it, and create a different, smaller group. Minus Cherri and Tiara.

Then I think about how Alicia basically caved and turned down Emilio because of them, and I drop her off the group too, so it's just Val and Everly.

"Thinking about going to the queer prom?"

Val responds first. "IDK, not really. You?"

I send a shrug emoji.

Everly: "Going with Lance?"

I cringe at the thought. After making out with Chris, what I had with Lance seems like an empty, pathetic joke. "No I don't think it's working out with him"

Everly: "Bummer but I get it." She starts typing again almost immediately. "You want to go to the dance to find someone else, I'd go with you." I heart her message. Even though that's not what I'm thinking about, I appreciate Everly supporting me like she always does.

Val: "What about the others?"

Me: "I rly don't think they'd be into it"

Everly: "Ya Cherri's not a fan. But it's your right to go Benji. I got your back if you want me there"

Me: "Thx Ev! Still deciding"

Val: "OK I'll think about it too"

It doesn't really help me decide whether I should actually go, but it helps slightly that they weren't both like "Are you crazy? Cherri would lose it." Which sounds silly once I think it to myself, but is also kind of what I was thinking would happen. Cherri can be really relentless once she gets an idea in her head, and can't let things go when one of us disagrees with her. I wouldn't call her a dictator, exactly, but ...

I go back and forth a dozen times on what to do next, but finally I opt for a half-assed kind of approach and text Chris. "Do you know about the GSA dance?"

I smoke some weed for courage while waiting for his response, which takes a few minutes.

"Yep." Another message comes soon after that: "I'm helping Jemma with it."

Jemma, of course. I keep forgetting that they seem to be friends, or at least acquaintances. I never even saw them together at my party; by the time I ran into Chris again later in the night, Jemma had already left as far as I could tell.

"You're going to it then?"

"I guess so." That's a kind of wishy washy response from someone who's helping organize it, I think.

"Are you going with someone?"

Chris doesn't answer for a minute, then: "IDK"

I stare at that unhelpful response. Is he hinting I should ask him? Is he putting me off because he's not ready to be out about being on a date with another guy? Does he have other prospects? I wish I could just straight-up ask him, but it feels impossible.

Especially since *I'm* not even sure I want to go as far as to be seen publicly with him. It's a social risk for me. I'm not proud of thinking that, but it's true. If I were sure we had something solid, maybe I'd be able to work up my nerve to risk pissing off Cherri, or having to endure insults from her and Tiara. But to put my reputation and popularity on the line for a guy who doesn't even know what his sexuality is, and who I've made out with all of two times? That just seems crazy, no matter *how* good it feels to kiss him.

Chris finally texts again. "Are you going?" Ugh. Even *that* doesn't have a simple answer.

"Not sure." That sounds too negative. "Maybe." I imagine him feeling as frustrated at my responses as I am at his.

"Wow we're so decisive!" I give that a "haha" reaction.

"I guess there's time to figure it out" I write, and he gives me a thumbs-up.

"More important tho" I add.

"???"

"When can I see you again?"

There's just enough of a pause for me to severely regret typing that and wish I could grab it back through the phone.

"Friday night?" Relief. Then excitement. Then nerves ... what'll we do? Where can we go? What do I tell my friends if they want to hang out that night? Then a little bit of sadness, because I feel like there's nobody I can tell about this.

But then the excitement crowds all of that out. I've got a date. I've got a fucking date!

CHAPTER EIGHTEEN: JEMMA

I am literally through the looking glass.

I'm not an idiot. The irony is not lost on me that a lot of people pretend to be straight while sneaking around with people of the same sex for fear of losing social status, and meanwhile I am doing the exact opposite.

If I knew of someone doing what I'm doing, pretending she's the queen bee of gayness, leading a meeting at the GSA to organize a gay dance that was her idea, all the while sneaking glances at one of the guys in the room and thinking about putting her hands all over him,

I'd be rolling my eyes so hard they'd probably pop out of my head. And yet here I am.

I feel like Chris and I are doing a fairly presentable job of not showing any visible interest in each other while we go through the motions of the tasks at hand. But I can't stop looking over at him when I think no one's watching. And I can't resist asking him to help me with the banners I ordered from the print shop that are in my car. And we can't stop smiling at each other as we walk, then jog, then race each other down the hall and out the door of the school into the parking lot.

And I can't help, after a careful look around at the deserted lot, pushing him into the backseat of my car and climbing on top of him, our hands roaming under each other's clothes as we kiss.

It's been going on like this for a little over a week and, while the hiding-everything part obviously adds some complications, there's something just so simple and fun about what we're doing. Chris has made no demands or even requests about defining what we are to each other or doing anything out in the open. He just follows my lead unquestioningly and treats me as a friend (I mean, when we're not sneaking off to make out).

Okay, maybe when he texts, there are a lot more heart emojis than a friend might normally send. Maybe some of the looks he gives me seem loaded with more than just lust. Maybe there's something a little emotionally ... significant-feeling about the way we've FaceTimed a couple times late at night when we're in our beds, talking until we start to get sleepy. And maybe I sometimes wish we could just hold hands when we're walking together in public.

But overall, it's another Friends With Benefits score, something to take my mind off the things that bother me, a little extra side fling to entertain me until I graduate. Although I have to admit my making out with Monica, which has happened a couple times since Chris and I first kissed, doesn't seem to have the same thrill compared with what I feel with him. But that's because he's a novelty, I tell myself, not because I feel something more for him than I do for Monica. How could I? He's just a guy, and I'm (mostly) a lesbian.

After school I head home to pick up some things and then to Brianna's place. She's been hinting at wanting to hang out outside of the GSA for a while, and she gave me and Monica puppydog eyes until we agreed to come to a sleepover.

She's got a girlfriend that she met over the summer at a theater camp, and apparently there's not much of an LGBTQ culture at her school. Brianna's told her a lot about our GSA and wants to have a "big gay sleepover" so she can meet some other lesbians. And so her girlfriend will know people besides her when they go to our queer prom. I mean, how could I say no to that?

So here I am, lugging pajamas, sleeping bag, and a toothbrush to a sophomore's house on a Friday night. Ugh. I try to swallow my negative attitude; it'll just make things worse. Forcing a smile, I knock on the door. Brianna greets me with a hug and a squeal and drags me inside to meet her girlfriend.

Trinity, I soon discover, is another excitable drama club type like Brianna, tall and skinny with a swoosh of short dyed pink hair that falls in her eyes a lot. The two of them have a crazy theater kid kind of love going on; it's adorable and a little annoying. I'm glad when the other guests arrive: Monica and Hope, an eleventh grader in the GSA.

It's weird at first, hanging out with them outside of school. I realize that with all the shit I've got going on, I haven't really been spending time with *anyone* recently. Like, Benji's party is the only one I've gone to this whole school year, and I've had the occasional hangout with Monica. Other than that, it's just been working at the bookstore, painting, planning for the dance, or stressing out over college shit.

But it ends up being a welcome relief to hang out with three underclassmen. And their big personalities keep things crazy and funny. Soon my stomach hurts and I have tears in my eyes from laughing. Even Monica, who's so even-keeled it drove me nuts (and bored me silly) when we were dating, is joining in on the silliness a little.

We're in Brianna's basement, which has a big room with games and a couch with a pullout bed and a plushy area rug on the concrete floor. Delivery pizzas come and are quickly consumed along with a ton of other junk food.

As the night goes on, hopped up on sugar, carbs, and caffeine, we jokingly try out some of the "scary" games that always seemed to pop up during middle-school sleepovers. First, four of us try to lift the fifth with two fingers each by chanting "light as a feather, stiff as a board." I've heard it's worked for people but it never has for me, and tonight is no exception. We try with Hope, then Monica, then Trinity, but no luck. Possibly because we can't all seem to keep a straight face at the same time.

Next we go into the bathroom (lights out) one by one to try and conjure Bloody Mary. That one legit still freaks me out, but I do it—I can't make seniors look bad! I mumble the name three times fast, the hairs on the back of my neck prickling uncomfortably as I stare at my indistinct face in the dark mirror, and run back with my heart pounding, laughing at myself but also *so* relieved to have gotten it over with.

We trade some classic urban legends and newer creepypasta stories, and all our laughter takes on a nervous pitch. Then Brianna goes to the games shelf and pulls out, from near the bottom, a dusty crumpled box. It's black with an image of two sets of hands on it, palms down, fingers touching a strangely shaped object. I start laughing as I recognize it. Hope's eyes get big. "Oh no. I've never messed with one of those before!"

"Come on, really?" Brianna says. "It's just a game! I don't believe in it, but it is kind of weird how it works." She pulls out the Ouija board and the sort of triangular white plastic thing and sets them on the coffee table in front of the couch.

"I believe in them," Trinity says semi-solemnly, "but I don't think the spirits in them are evil, so I'll do it."

Monica and I exchange glances and shrugs. I've played with one a few times in maybe eighth or ninth grade; half the time you get nonsense letters and numbers, and the other half, the answers are so spot-on that I think it's people's subconscious causing them to move to the letters they want. But either way, it is a fun, eerie feeling when it seems like you're not doing anything and it just starts to move under your hands.

Brianna can't convince Hope, but she perches on the couch where she can see the board as the rest of us gather around it, two on either side of the coffee table, and place our hands on the plastic piece in the middle.

"Spirit, are you there?" Brianna tries to sound serious but we can tell she's trying not to crack up.

There's a pause, and then just as I think maybe we're all too old and skeptical for our subconscious minds to override our disbelief, it starts to move, creeping ever so slowly over to "Yes." Hope and Trinity both gasp. I hold in my snickering because it's more fun if you pretend to take it seriously.

Trinity is next. "Spirit, what is your name?" The thing doesn't wait as long to start moving this time, gliding to the M, then A, then X.

"Max," we all say when it rests on the third letter without moving.

"Max, are you a male spirit?" Brianna asks.

"No," Max indicates after hesitating for a tiny bit, and we're all super happy that we've got some female energy coming from the spirit world.

The questions flood in after that, mostly from Brianna and Trinity, a lot of yes-no questions about future careers, fame, wealth, and so on.

"We should ask something about the dance," Trinity says. She's brought it up several times during the party and is obviously excited about it.

"Ooh!" Brianna exclaims. "We should ask Max who Hope is gonna get with at the dance!"

"No!" shrieks Hope. "Don't get my name involved with spirits. What if they come haunt me later?"

"Oh fine." Brianna sounds disappointed.

Trinity grins. "Let's do Jemma then." Possibly she's oblivious to me and Monica being exes sitting right next to each other, or maybe she just thinks it's old news. Or maybe she's hopped up on Mountain Dew and not thinking. Anyway, before I can figure out a way to object without sounding weird or defensive, she jumps in. "Max, who is Jemma gonna hook up with at the queer prom?"

The piece is slower to get going this time, maybe because of the four people touching it, at least two of their subconscious minds want nothing to do with this awkwardness. But it does lurch into motion at last, and creeps over to the C. My stomach does a nervous little flip at that. Max is feeling decisive now, because the plastic thing scoots more quickly to the right, over to the H. It's not my subconscious that causes me to put a little resistance on it with my hands—I know exactly what I'm doing—but I don't want to be obvious so I don't hold back very much, and my hesitation is soon overruled. H it is.

"C, H …" Hope, who's been watching with rapt attention, sounds thoughtful. Then she squeals in disgust. "Ugh! What if it's trying to say 'Cherri'?"

Brianna and Monica both burst out laughing. Trinity looks from one to the other. "Who's that?"

"Oh, she's the literal worst!" Hope says.

"Yeah, she's kind of a nightmare," Monica agrees in her matter-of-fact way, and that sets Brianna and Hope into fits of laughter.

"And she is like the one person in the whole school I can absolutely guarantee will *not* be attending queer prom," I say with finality.

"Well then, who is it, Max?" Trinity turns our attention back to the board. The pointer, which had politely paused during our outburst, starts to veer left and slightly downward to the second row of letters. Toward the letter R. This time I try to put the brakes on a little harder, but it's no use; it's clear where it's going.

I pull my hands off the piece and everyone stops and looks at me.

"I … I'm kind of bored with this. Can we just watch a show instead?"

I know it's pretty obvious I wanted to stop for some other reason, but no one says anything. Trinity promises we can stop as long as I put my hands back on the thing so we can say goodbye to the spirit and make sure the portal to the other world is properly closed. I go along with it and no one tries to push for getting the other question's answer finished first.

Brianna and Trinity push the coffee table out of the way and take the pullout couch; the rest of us spread out a little on the thick rug between the sofa bed and the TV. Brianna flips through the options on her TV and settles on a cute queer teen romcom, and we all get in our sleeping bags and start to settle down.

The others keep chattering away, but for me, the fun of the night has been sucked away. Honestly I'd rather leave and sleep in my own bed, but I don't want to make a big scene so I just lay quietly in my sleeping bag, pretending to have dozed off. The more I think about what went down with the Ouija board, the more pissed off I feel. I now know Brianna has seen something or guessed something about me and Chris, and she picked a truly shitty way to let me know. I don't know her *that* well, but I thought she was better than this.

And I can't figure out what her angle is; she's always been nice to me. I thought she liked me—why would she invite me over if she didn't?—but it seems like she just wants to stir up some cheap shitty drama. What a fucking typical sophomore thing to do.

At the same time, though, it makes me wonder … what do I have to lose if people *do* find out? I mean, Monica may get pissed at me; some people might, I guess, think I was fake gay or something … but I'm going to be out of here soon anyway. I'm definitely not going to go to college anywhere near the rest of these people, so what would be the harm in coming out as dating a guy for the last few months in my high school career? Gradually, my anger subsides, and I start thinking that maybe, in the end, this will turn out to be for the best. Chris and I can finally stop hiding. I lie awake a while longer, eyes closed, smiling a little up at the darkness, imagining it all being so much simpler.

CHAPTER NINETEEN: CHRIS

The mall is busy and loud. A fake Santa sits in the rotunda amid crowds of holiday shoppers, a line of kids waiting to sit on his lap. I'm waiting for Jemma, who told me to meet her here after she gets off work. I don't know why; she's never asked me to be in public with her, not since that night at Crush. I wander around, people-watching and checking my phone occasionally. Finally a message comes in. "I'm here, meet me at the food court"

I catch sight of her immediately when I get there. Her curls are tied up in a neater than usual bun for work and she's got on a black coat that comes almost down to her knees. She looks perfect and adorable. She glances around, biting her lip a little, until she spots me.

I hurry over to her, a big grin already on my face—I just can't help it when I'm around her. She's smiling too, and I feel like she's looking at me more directly than she ever has at school or when anyone is around.

"Thanks for meeting me."

"No problem!"

A little silence stretches between us. "How was work?" I ask.

"Pretty good. Busy because of Christmas, you know." She cocks her head. "Anyway, I wondered if you would let me buy you dinner and a movie?"

My mouth almost drops open at that. "Uh, yeah!" I wasn't sure what this was going to be about, but I made sure that I'm not expected home anytime soon.

She grins. "We've got about forty minutes until the movie starts, so fast food okay?"

"Yeah, of course!"

She lets me choose the place. I pick Chinese and get sweet-and-sour chicken; she gets some kind of noodles with tofu. We take our plastic trays to a table that's a little bit off to the side, but we're still in public, so I make sure not to get too clingy or close to her. I've definitely sensed that she doesn't want people to know about us. I think it's just because she's figuring out her own sexuality. Well, I tell myself that, but some part of me also worries sometimes that it's because she doesn't want to be seen with me because, well, why would she?

But here we are! Even if we're just hanging out as friends, clearly she's not *too* worried about being seen in public with me—that's promising!

Jemma asks me how things are going, and I talk about my grandpa a little bit, though there isn't much to say; I still haven't gone to see him at the home. I think my parents want to push me more, but nobody has yet, not even my grandma, so I'm kind of just putting it off, I don't know for how long. But I hear from my mom that he's about the same as he was when they put them in there. Not very aware of his surroundings or anything that's happened for the past several years; it's like he's living in the past.

I manage to talk about him pretty calmly but when I think about that part—about him living in a time when maybe I wasn't even born yet—I do get a little choked up. Jemma reaches her hand across the table. Her slender, delicate fingers touch mine, brushing them lightly at first and then linking together with them so we're holding hands on top of the table. My heart starts pounding and I forget to be sad. I look down at our hands and then at Jemma.

"So …" She's got this little smile on her face. "I wanted to ask you something." I can't tell what she's thinking. "I was wondering if you'd consider—" she takes a deep breath, biting her lip again. She's so cute when she does that.

"Consider …?"

"Well, I was thinking maybe we could … go to the dance together?"

"Ohhh." My mind is racing … she can't possibly mean what I want her to mean. I hesitate.

She shrugs, still smiling a little. "Like, you know, as a date, kind of."

My stomach aches with excitement. I can't believe she's saying this to me. It's so amazing to think that we might not have to hide anymore. But I only celebrate internally for a second before another big realization hits me: If we're going to be together openly, what does that mean for me and Benji?

He hasn't exactly seemed like he wanted to be public about us either, but we've been getting closer and closer. We've even been on what I guess you could call a date; he drove us out to a restaurant in the suburbs and bought me dinner, and afterwards we walked around the same lake that we had the morning after his party. It was freezing cold this time, not just chilly, but we re-enacted our kiss—in the dark this time, with no nosy lady jogger interrupting us—and then I came back to his place, where we went farther than we ever had before.

So I still don't quite know what we're doing, but our texts are a hundred percent flirty now, and when we see each other at school it's kind of like with Jemma; we exchange stealthy smiles and glances like we've got the best-kept secret in the world. What's going to become of that secret if Jemma and I go to the dance together?

I want this so bad, but I also love what I have with Benji, and somehow I wish that could be more. What the fuck is wrong with me?

Jemma's looking at me and I realize I haven't said anything in a while. "Sorry … I'm genuinely speechless." I laugh and she joins in, looking relieved. "I mean—that sounds—but what about Monica?"

Jemma winces a little bit, nodding. "Well … I think you probably know that even though we're not going out anymore, I have made out with Monica a few times recently. It doesn't mean anything," she adds quickly. "I mean, it's just kind of a physical thing. I don't feel the same way about her that I used to. But I think

… I think I'm going to stop doing that. And anyway"—she laughs a little—"I think once she finds out about us, she won't wanna keep doing it anyway." Jemma looks down at the table then back up at me. "I don't feel the same about her as I do about you." She's actually blushing for once; usually I'm the one turning red all the time!

I fumble for words. I want to tell her how into her I am, but I'm also feeling so guilty about Benji. She just told me about Monica, so in a way it's the perfect time to come clean … but the way she talked about Monica doesn't sound like there's anything there. I really don't think I can say the same thing about me and Benji. And what does that mean, if I like her *and* I like him—does it mean I have to choose one of them somehow? Maybe one reason I've been so chill about both of them wanting to keep us a secret is because it was a way for me to justify being with both of them.

If Jemma wants to get serious with me, then it's a whole other situation. "This is a lot to take in." I take a deep breath. "I really really like

you, but—" I scrub my hand over my face "—
it's so complicated. I don't wanna do the
wrong thing."

I know I'm saying true things but I also
know I'm leaving out a lot. I keep feeling more
and more guilty as I talk. I think she assumes
it's just about Monica and her public sexuality,
because she smiles reassuringly. "It *is*
complicated. I personally don't want to
overthink it anymore—I've been doing that for
too long—but I totally understand that you
need to think about it. I know it's a weird
situation so, you know, take your time. We've
got time." She squeezes my hand. "Don't
worry about it if it stresses you out; we don't
have to do it. It was just an idea. I just felt like,
you know, I've been kind of treating you as a
convenience or something, and it's important
to me that you know you're way more than
that."

My heart is turning cartwheels. Guilt is
momentarily eclipsed by intense excitement
and happiness as it washes over me that
Jemma really likes me! "Okay." I try to sound

calm but I know I don't. "Let me try to figure out what I think about everything."

She's still smiling. "Okay, it's a deal. Still wanna go to the movies with me?"

"Of course! And not just cause you're buying either."

She laughs. We finish eating and walk to the other side of the mall where the movie theater is. She's picked a scary movie about a haunted house and a little kid who's the only one who can see the spirits. It has lots of jump scares, aka reasons to touch each other. The movie starts out good but kind of loses my attention … or maybe it's because of Jemma's hand on my thigh.

I'm glad we're sitting near the back of the theater; hopefully not many people see us as one kiss turns into another. Pretty soon all I can think about is touching and kissing Jemma, listening to her quiet little gasps as I run my hand up under her shirt. The movie ends and the lights go up. Jemma takes a mirror out of her purse, laughs at her reflection, and fixes her lipstick as best she can before we head out into the lobby, wiping my lips for me as well so they're not quite as obviously stained with red.

Jemma holds my hand as we leave. It's the first time that's ever happened, and it's almost more exciting than what we were doing in the theater. We keep exchanging looks that last way too long, smiling and shaking our heads.

The rest of the mall is closed, so the theater only lets us exit straight into the parking lot. My car is actually pretty close since I didn't know where we would start out in the mall, so we run to it and I get the heater going. We make out some more as the car warms up. Then she directs me where to drive to take her to her car.

There's one sit-down restaurant sort of attached to the outside of the mall, and it's the only other thing that's open right now. Jemma's car is parked in the front row right near it, so I pull up next to it. She starts to get out. "Wait!" She looks at me questioningly. I jump out of the car and run around to her side, open her door, and hold out my hand.

She laughs and takes it, and I help her out. "How very old-fashioned of you."

"I know I'm being stupid. I just … thank you for this amazing date." She leans against my car, smiling up at me, and I can't resist kissing her once again, squeezing her slight little body under the thick layers of her sweater and coat.

There's a burst of laughter and voices as the door to the restaurant opens. Jemma doesn't even pull away and I don't either for a second. Then I recognize a male voice. I jump away from Jemma, my heart in my throat, and turn. It's Benji, Cherri, and the rest of the mean girls.

The girls haven't really noticed us yet, but Benji is staring right at me. The look on his face makes me wish I could disappear. One by one his friends notice him standing frozen with big shocked eyes, and they all turn curiously in the direction he's looking. One of the girls—I can't remember her name—says "Benji, what's—" Her eyes dart between me and her friend, and it seems like a little realization dawns on her.

I step toward him, wondering what Jemma thinks—what everyone thinks. "Benji …" I can't think what should come next.

"Oh my god." He sounds dazed. "Not again." He turns and hurries away. A few of his friends follow, but Cherri and Tiara stare at me a little longer. Cherri's got an odd expression on her face, somewhere between disgust and fury. I want to run after Benji, but Jemma's right here. I don't know what to do. I look at her reluctantly. "Jemma, I—"

"Chris?" Her eyes get faraway for a second and then she focuses on me again. "Oh, right. Benji. This whole time you—" Her face starts to crumple as if she's going to cry, then hardens. "Wow, I am a fucking idiot. I can't believe what I was about to give up to be with you." She shakes her head. "Well, that was close." There's a hard edge of cynicism in her voice. "Don't feel like you need to come to the GSA anymore. Your boyfriend wouldn't approve anyway, or his friends." She turns her back on me, gets in her car, and drives away, the engine complaining that she hasn't warmed it up.

The air seems even colder with everyone gone except Cherri and Tiara, who are now whispering to one another while they stare. I get back in my car, starting the ignition with shaking hands. My whole body is numb and my mind is mostly blank except a vague sense of dread like I get in nightmares sometimes. When the numbness passes and I feel my stomach aching, I wish I could go back to the shock where I couldn't feel anything. I get home and lie on my bed in my clothes with my eyes shut. But there's no turning off the movie projector in my mind replaying the awful scene over and over again. There's nothing I can do but let misery wash over me and wait for sleep, which doesn't come until there's already a hint of gray daylight in the sky.

CHAPTER TWENTY: BENJI

Why why why? It's all I can think. Why did I let myself get sucked once again into falling for some guy, thinking he could actually like me back, when of course he's not gay, just like Lance isn't really gay. Hell, even Jemma isn't really gay. I'm probably the only actual fucking queer in our entire school.

Val and Everly don't say much on the way home, and when they do it's not about him or me or what just happened. Thank god we'd come to the restaurant in two separate cars so I don't have to ride with Cherri. Not after seeing the look on her face as she figured out what was going on. I don't want to deal with her judgment and her ridicule. Not only did I let myself get humiliated once again by a guy choosing a girl over me, but this time it was Chris fucking Quinn, the biggest loser in our entire grade.

The ride home is bad, but being alone after they drop me off is even worse. All I can do is go over and over all the moments between Chris and me, all the texts we sent, second-guessing every single one of them for the sick empty jokes that they were. I cannot believe I almost asked him to the dance. Thank god that didn't happen at least. I take an edible hoping I can forget about everything that's happened, but it just makes things worse. My brain spirals even more out of control. Every part of my place reminds me of Chris; the game room where I found him drunk and silly after everyone else had left my party, the couch where he slept that night. And my bed; god. I feel like I can still smell his cologne on my pillow.

The next morning I head up to the main house. I find my mom and dad in the living room. They look surprised to see me, which makes me kind of sad as I think about how I've been spending barely any time there these past couple months. But they don't make a big deal about it. My dad's on his laptop and my mom's reading a book. I make room to sit on the couch by shoving aside some piles of magazines.

Mom smiles at me. "So, Benji, are you going to that dance after winter break?"

My stomach drops. Of course she knows about that; she volunteers for the school with a bunch of other parents. "I don't know. Probably not."

"Why not?" She frowns. "Maybe it'd be good for you to spend some time with … other people for a change." I know she doesn't really care for my friend group and preferred when I hung out with GSA kids.

I think about all the stuff she doesn't know; about Cherri being super against the queer prom, about my fake whatever-it-was with

Chris. I don't feel like getting into any of it. "I'll think about it."

We don't talk much after that; they get back to what they're doing and I just scroll mindlessly on my phone. But it feels nice to be around my parents. Even though I moved out of the main house for a reason, I do miss living with them in some ways.

I spend most of the day lounging around the living room. I see some texts pop up from my friends—a couple from Chris too—but I ignore them. I turn off notifications so I won't see if any more come in. I don't want to deal with Cherri's ridicule and I don't want to hear whatever Chris has to say about why he did what he did.

In the late afternoon, the doorbell rings out of nowhere. We're all kind of shocked. There's plenty of "no soliciting" and "do not ring" signs on our front door, and my parents never have friends over. No one would just show up unannounced.

We look at each other and mutually, silently agree to just wait until the person goes away. Then the ringing comes again. My mom looks at me. "Benji?" I hate the kind of fearful look in her eye and the tightness in my dad's jaw.

"Yeah mom, I'll take care of it." I go to the door. As I get near it, the bell rings again, insistently this time, followed by loud knocking.

I'm already pissed off when I open the door a crack, but my reaction turns to shock when I see Cherri standing there. And she looks even more pissed than I feel. "I've been texting you all day. Why are you fucking ghosting me?"

"I'm not, I just—"

"How long have you been going out with this fucking guy? And I just heard that you were thinking about going to the fake prom too? God. I thought I was your friend and you've been hiding all this shit from me."

"I don't have to tell you everything." I try to keep the nervousness out of my voice. "You know you can be kind of … judgy and, I don't know, controlling, right? Like how you basically told Alicia she can't see Emilio?"

Cherri folds her arms. "I just say what I think. I would never tell anyone what they can and can't do—that's up to them."

"Well it doesn't come off that way."

Her exhale sounds like a laugh, but she's not smiling. "How long have you been feeling that way? Have you basically been pretending to be my friend this whole fucking time? Do you think I'm just like a total bitch?"

She doesn't wait for a response. "Let me in. We need to talk about this."

"I can't—" I try to think of a way to turn the conversation away from her coming in, but my mind's a blank.

"Benji, what the fuck? Just let me in." She pushes her way past me. The door opens wider into the empty hallway, and she takes off down it without looking back. I follow her quickly but it's too late. She stops at the living room entrance. "Oh my *god*." I catch up to her and look in. I had my own moment of fresh shock when I came in this morning after not having seen it for a while, but seeing it through Cherri's eyes, it's much much worse.

We've got a big living room, huge really, with giant windows, but they all have heavy curtains that stay closed, so very little natural light comes in. All around the edges, piles of boxes, magazines, newspapers, and other unidentifiable stuff are heaped everywhere. In the middle there's a few chairs and a couch, but even those are stacked high with magazines and newspapers. Cherri's face turns from shock to a mean delight. A cruel smile curls her lips.

"Wow, Benji, you've been hiding even more than I thought from me." She pulls out her phone and before I can react she's filming, turning in a small circle and capturing every detail of our living room.

"Cherri, stop!" I rush toward her but she darts away from me out into the hallway. She runs from room to room with me in pursuit, getting video of my mom's craft room, the kitchen, the bathroom. She dashes upstairs and finds my parents' room too. Every room except my dad's study is stuffed with piles of clothes, packages that have never even been opened, toys that I outgrew ten years ago that I used to beg my mom to get rid of. Until I gave up and moved out.

"Cherri please, you can't do this!" But she's put her phone away in her purse, which she holds to her chest. I don't feel like I can fight her for it so I just stand there helplessly.

"You're such a fake, Benji." The disgust in Cherri's voice is like my worst nightmare coming true. She runs back downstairs and I hear the front door slam. When I reach the living room again, my parents stare at me, horrified. My dad looks sick with worry. "Was she taking pictures of our house?"

I nod, feeling nauseous myself.

"She would never show them to anyone, would she? She's your friend!"

"I'll talk to her." I'm not feeling hopeful but I head toward my car, texting as I go.

"Cherri I need to talk to you. I know you're mad at me but please don't drag my parents into this. let's talk OK?"

No response. I call but it goes straight to voicemail. I reach my car and text her one more time. "Cherri, please!"

I finally see her typing back. The text pops in, chilling and short. "check my TikTok asshole"

I slump in the car seat and open the app. There it is; jerky footage of my parents' house, panning around to capture the overwhelming amounts of clutter, zooming in on piles of rubble; there's even a shot of my dad looking like he's seen a ghost. Cherri's got loads of followers, of course, so I watch the views, shares, and comments piling up. I turn my phone off and put my head down on the steering wheel.

Finally I get out of my car since there's no sense going to Cherri's now. I drag my feet on the way back to the house to tell my parents what's happened. At my dad's insistence I send Cherri a couple more texts, begging her to take the TikTok down, but I know she won't. I finally return to my place. Not like I can relax

there either, but I don't want to see my parents'
scared and angry faces anymore.

CHAPTER TWENTY-ONE: JEMMA

Going through the motions of life instead of really living it is actually pretty easy, once I accept what a sick joke it all is.

Luckily there's only one week of school left after the thing with Chris. The sonnet promotion goes just as well as we hoped, and we sell a ton of tickets to the prom. Some of the invitations cause a little drama, but it's nothing compared to the drama that I brought into my world. It unfolds around me like a mildly interesting show I'm not really watching.

We have one more GSA meeting before winter break and Chris has the good sense not to show up. The other people in the club keep their distance from me like I'm some kind of pariah. I can't tell if it's because Brianna told everyone what she had figured out about me and Chris, or if it was just word getting around from Benji's friends about what they saw outside the mall. It doesn't really matter either way.

Even Monica barely looks at or talks to me beyond what's strictly necessary. We have a few planning things to finish up before winter break starts, and then we'll be ready for the dance in the new year.

I spend the break picking up extra hours at the bookstore and doing nothing much at home. I bake and eat a lot of cookies. The sugar doesn't boost my mood; it just takes away my appetite for any real food. Even painting, which is the one thing I always had to help me process whatever was going on in my life, seems to have deserted me. Blank canvases lean against the wall of my bedroom, gathering dust. I have zero inspiration to pick up a paintbrush.

My mom is seeing a guy, and I guess they're getting pretty serious. When she's not working, she's usually out with him, so I have the house to myself.

Chris tries to contact me from time to time. I ignore his texts, delete his voicemails without listening to them, block him on social media. I don't spend much time on my phone anyway over the break. When I do, I see that there's been some kind of scandal with Benji's parents turning out to be massive hoarders.

At first I feel a kind of mean pleasure thinking about Benji getting humiliated, but that doesn't last long. Judging from his face that night, he didn't know Chris was sneaking around with me any more than I knew Chris was getting with him.

It looks like Cherri's the one who spilled the hoarding secret. I wonder if it's because of the Chris thing somehow; she looked pretty pissed that night, though I assumed at the time it was directed at Chris. But I don't have the energy to think too hard about that, and eventually I just shut off social media entirely.

Christmas comes and goes. Me and my mom get each other a couple of presents. Christmas Day itself is pretty low-key; it has been for years but this year it's even more subdued. Mom's guy comes over for dinner. His name is Greg and he's a tattoo artist at the studio next to the salon where my mom works. He seems nice and I try to be happy for my mom, but it's hard to feel much of anything.

New Year's Eve creeps up. I ignore texts from Brianna inviting me to some kind of celebration at her house. I still haven't been able to decide what her deal is, ever since she used the Ouija board to basically mess with me and try to expose what I was doing with Chris. I have no idea why she'd want me to come over; just so she could gloat at how stupid I was to get involved with a guy and then get tricked and humiliated by him?

Anyway, I'm not sure anyone else at her party would want me around. I don't imagine anyone in the GSA has much respect for me anymore; hell, *I* don't have much respect for me anymore.

My mom has plans to go out with Greg for New Year's. She leaves a bottle of sparkling wine in the fridge. "I'm not gonna condone underage drinking or anything, but if something happens to that bottle I'll look the other way," she tells me.

"Thanks, Mom." I try to smile convincingly.

"Are you sure you're okay being alone tonight, sweetheart?"

"Yeah, I'm fine." I've been trying really hard not to look too depressed, telling her I just need to rest after all the dance planning and college stuff. I know she's worried; she can tell there's something more going on. But eventually she goes off on her date.

I break open the sparkling wine after dinner. With a whole bottle to myself, I'm already pretty tipsy when midnight approaches. I open a streaming version of the local news on my phone to watch the countdown. Usually they have a bunch of the news anchors reporting from different parts of the city; this year is no different, though I notice Benji's dad isn't taking part like he usually does. I feel a pang of pity for the guy, even though I never thought much about him one way or the other before.

Midnight comes, the least momentous New Year's ever for me. I watch a few more minutes of the newscasters saying inane stupid things about resolutions, and interviewing partiers to get *their* inane stupid thoughts about resolutions.

I tap my phone to close out the livestream. Just as I do, a FaceTime request pops up and I accidentally hit the green button to accept it. Suddenly Chris's face fills my phone screen. He's got that haunted, bruised-under-the-eyes look, kind of like he had that day in the guidance counselor's office.

He looks really surprised that I picked up. "Hey Jemma."

I roll my eyes. "Okay, you got me. Here I am. What is it you want to say to me, Chris?"

His words come out in a rush; I suppose he's been waiting to say them for a long time. "I just really really want to apologize. I get why you don't want to talk to me, but I just felt like

I needed you to know how really sorry I am about everything." He takes a deep breath. "I've been the biggest asshole and I just wanted to—"

I cut him off. "You know what? It's fine. It was a terrible decision to kiss you, and every decision I've made since then has been completely inadvisable. So it's actually really great that you snapped me out of that, you know?" His face kind of flinches with every word that I say. Part of me wants to feel bad for him, but I mostly feel glad I'm hurting him.

"You really wish we hadn't …?" He starts timidly and trails off.

I laugh bitterly. "Well gee, what do you think? Obviously I'm just a terrible judge of character. I misjudged *you* completely. And you're not the only one; there's been a lot of other people that I managed to be wrong about recently. So yeah, I'm glad it's all over."

He looks down as if he's trying to find words, but I keep going. "It's great, really. The rest of my life is a disaster too, so I'm glad everything is so consistent."

"What do you mean?"

I pause, wondering if I'm really about to say what else has been weighing on me. "Well, it turns out, it's not just everyone around me who's been pretending to be something they're not. I've been doing it too."

"What do you mean?" he says again, confused.

I drain my glass of champagne and go to the kitchen for another one. "I'm not going to college."

"What?" He wasn't expecting that, I can tell.

"I never even applied." I turn the bottle upside down, shaking the last few drops of wine into my glass. "The deadline for most of the places I wanna go to is almost here, and I don't have anything done." I can hear myself slurring my words as they pour out. "I know. I've been pretending to everyone that I was on top of this, and it got harder and harder to ask for any help so I just … let it slip. I just didn't do anything about it, and now it's too late, and I guess I'll be working at the fucking bookstore when I'm done with high school, and that's it! The end of Jemma Matthews the honors student, the artist, the lesbian role model. Every single thing people thought about me was a lie. So when I think about it that way, Chris, how can I even be mad at you?"

"Jemma … I know this is my fault too. If I hadn't done such a terrible thing, you probably could've gotten your applications done over the break."

"Who knows?" I say flippantly. "It's too late now so it doesn't really matter. Anyway, I've gotta go. Happy new year or whatever." I shut off FaceTime and his sad worried face disappears. I feel relief but also just a small twinge of longing. Okay, maybe not so small. There's no sense wishing that things were back to the way they were when the way they were was a joke, but the mind doesn't always listen to common sense.

The winter break had been dragging on forever, but all of a sudden it's over and I get this hollow feeling in the pit of my stomach. It's time to go back to school, and it's time to put on this fucking dance whether I like it or not.

At least it's better at school than it was that last week before winter break. I think by finally accepting that I've just completely fucked myself on college applications, I've got a certain fatalistic attitude that's helping me deal with everything. The GSA is frantic with last-minute preparation for the dance, but I find myself the calm center of everything: organizing people, assigning tasks, getting everything together.

The first Friday of the new semester, we have one more after-school meeting and then everyone goes home for a couple of hours before the dance. Monica and I are the last ones to leave the classroom. She falls into step next to me. "Hey Jemma, can I ask you something?"

I nod, not sure what this is about. We haven't talked privately at all since break ended.

"Would you go to the prom with me?" I stop and we stare at each other in the empty hallway.

"Are you serious?" I try to read her face. "After everything? God, why would you even want to be seen with an asshole like me? I'm basically a joke."

"Listen, Jemma." Monica puts her hand on my shoulder, and I can tell it's not a romantic gesture. "I knew about you and Chris pretty much from when he joined the GSA."

I can't even process that. "What?"

"Oh my god, it was so obvious to me that you guys liked each other." She smiles a little. "Who do you think did the thing with the Ouija board? Pretty funny, right?"

My mouth drops open. I can't believe I've been blaming Brianna this whole time. "But why did you—"

She shrugs. "I admit I was a little bit pissed; it was halfway between joking and trying to get revenge on you. But I'm not mad anymore. You were always honest with me after we broke up—at least about how you felt about me. You never led me on. So even though you hid the thing with Chris, I couldn't really feel betrayed." I don't know what to say. This is the first time since it all went down that I've even allowed myself to imagine that everyone doesn't completely hate me.

"People get it, Jemma. Sexuality is complicated." Monica laughs. "This isn't, like, I don't know, when some far right Christian dude gets caught in bed with another guy. It's just you figuring out your stuff, and nobody is going to judge you for that, at least not anyone who matters."

I start to cry a little bit. I didn't realize how much I've been holding back. She hugs me. "So what do you say? Do you have a dress for this thing, or a suit maybe? How about we get fancy and go together? Just as friends."

"You're so amazing, Monica," I say when I can talk again. "I have completely underestimated you this whole time."

"Thanks, but … I could've been a lot clearer with you before now."

"I'm just so glad we're talking now." I wipe tears off my cheeks. "So yeah, I'd be honored to go to the dance with you if you really want to."

"Of course I do! Why else would I ask you?"

I feel my lip quivering but I give a shaky laugh. "I'll go get ready and meet you in the gym in like an hour?"

"It's a date!" But her smile tells me she's kidding.

CHAPTER TWENTY-TWO: CHRIS

Winter break is just ten thousand kinds of awful this year. Benji won't answer any of my texts or calls. Jemma does pick up that one time on New Year's Eve, but it's almost worse than not talking to her at all. My brother and sister are home from college and I guess they found out about some of what happened, even though I didn't tell them anything.

They kind of go back and forth between teasing me about being a player and trying to lend me a sympathetic ear. Neither is helpful. No one can make me feel better about what I did to Benji and Jemma, and my life seems empty without them. It was an amazing couple of months but now it seems like it couldn't have been real. And I have absolutely no one to blame but myself.

My parents finally drag me and my siblings to see my grandpa in the nursing home the day after Christmas. We can't all squeeze into his room so Grandma brings him out in a wheelchair. I guess he's been falling so much that it's just better that way. He sits slumped over, barely acknowledging our presence, sometimes mumbling things I can't really understand—his side of conversations that he's reliving, maybe.

He seems upset the whole time, confused and lost. It's even worse than I thought it would be. I sit as far away as I can without my parents noticing what I'm doing and try not to look at him too closely.

I think about the time I spent at his house, the music and games and jokes. Even that stupid cigarillo incident seems like the most fun I ever had. Maybe if I hadn't avoided seeing him in the home for this long, I would've gotten a little bit of the old Grandpa before he went away completely, but I'll never know and now there's just another empty space in my life where his love used to be.

So that's Christmastime, and then there's my miserable call with Jemma, and the break is pretty much over.

I go back to school but not to the GSA, of course. I feel bad because I had volunteered to do a few things for the dance, but I don't want to bother Jemma or make her think I'm fucking with her or stalking her or anything. I figure she'd much rather find someone else to pick up the slack than have to put up with my presence at all.

I see her and Benji occasionally in the hall but I always look away. I avoid Benji in the one class we share, too. They've made it clear they don't want to see me, so the least I can do is respect that. Besides, they've both got way bigger things on their minds than my awful behavior; I know Jemma's got to be worried about the college situation, even if she pretended not to care on our call, and of course everyone knows what Benji's family is going through since Cherri posted that video of his house. I wish there was something I could do to help, but the only thing I have to offer is staying out of their way.

Marty meets me after school for a ride home on Friday as usual. Seeing him a couple times over break was like my only source of comfort. We didn't talk about any of the stuff that had happened to me. I don't know if he heard everything; it seems like gossip spread through the school pretty quickly, but Marty never pays much attention to things like that. We just continue our usual routine, playing games or watching seventies and eighties movies while he smokes weed. It's soothingly familiar.

He leans his head against the window as we're pulling out of the school parking lot, looking like he's daydreaming, so I don't see it coming when he speaks up. "Hey, are you taking anyone to the dance tonight?"

That came out of nowhere. I figured he probably didn't even really know about the dance or remember it was tonight. "I don't think I'm going." I try to sound like I'm not interested. Try not to think about me and Benji texting about whether we would go. Try not to think about Jemma inviting me to be her date.

Marty sits up, looking alert all of a sudden. "You worked your ass off on that, man. Like, way more than I've ever done for anything."

"Well, *that's* not hard to beat."

Marty laughs but doesn't drop it. "You gotta go to that dance. You earned it."

"I don't know." I tap the steering wheel. "I think I pissed off a lot of people that'll be there."

Something about the way Marty looks at me tells me maybe he *does* know what's been going on. "Well, *I'm* going. I'd have a way better time if you came with me, though. Like, I won't even know anybody else there, I don't think."

I think about it. I know Jemma will be there, though I have no idea about Benji. Wouldn't it ruin their night if I showed up? But maybe if I just leave them alone, or if I quickly apologize to them and then stay out of their way, maybe it would be all right. I mean we have a whole semester of school we need to get through; I can't just avoid them completely forever.

"Well, if you need a wingman, I guess I could go." I try to keep my tone casual. "But you can't wear that stupid fucking poncho, okay buddy?"

Marty's eyes widen. "No way, man! I got this fucking fly seventies suit at a thrift store over the break. Don't worry—you're gonna have the hottest date there."

We both crack up at that, the first time I've actually laughed in a long time. This could be the worst idea ever, but I feel weirdly energized and … lighter somehow.

CHAPTER TWENTY-THREE: BENJI

Compared to the excruciating week before winter break—dragging myself to school after my humiliation by Chris and then Cherri—and the holidays, which I basically spend in isolation, coming back to school isn't that bad. There's fewer stares, less whispering that stops suddenly when I come into sight. The weird trolls on social media have moved on to some other target. I'm just kind of numb.

I keep my head down and try to get through the days as quietly and painlessly as possible. I say hi to Val, Everly, and Alicia when I see them in the halls, but since they're still hanging out with Cherri and Tiara, I leave it at that.

Being able to avoid Chris for a few weeks, it was easier to convince myself I hadn't really cared about him. Seeing him again hurts. He looks as lost and sad as I feel, honestly. If he was trying to be a player, he did a pretty poor job of it. Even as pissed as I am, sometimes I almost feel bad for him. But then I remind myself that I was just some weird game for him.

I'm lonely, but I can't even begin to imagine trying to make new friends or deal with what happened between me and Cherri. All through winter break I had to watch my parents deal with the shitstorm she started, which of course spread past TikTok into local news and all those sites that specialize in shocking stories of successful people turning out to be pathetic losers. My dad had stopped fighting my mom's hoarding a long time ago and learned to live with it, but now it's like old wounds have been reopened. It feels like he barely speaks to

Mom—from what little I've seen. I spend even less time in the main house now.

At least with a couple of washes, Chris's cologne scent is now completely gone from my sheets. I Febreze the hell out of my other furniture until there's no trace of it anywhere in my place.

The day of the queer prom approaches and it's gotten kind of hot, which I didn't expect. I don't know if the scandal of Jemma the great lesbian savior being into guys, and Chris the random weirdo turning out to be a two-timing bisexual, kind of gave the dance a weird social allure. Maybe it was going to be popular anyway. But for whatever reason, it seems like it's all anybody's talking about in the day or two leading up to it.

I try not to think about it, though. Friday afternoon I crash on my couch in front of the TV with half an edible to take the edge off. The combination of mindless screens and THC get me to, if not a happy place, at least a resigned place. Chasing popularity over the past year felt like it was going to take me somewhere, but it was actually just kind of tiring. I don't miss it much. But I do kind of miss my friends, even Cherri and Tiara. They were awful a lot of the time, but I have to admit they could also be really fun.

I'm almost dozing off when I hear my doorbell ring. Thinking it might be my mom—although why she wouldn't call first I'm not sure—I go to the door. When I see Cherri standing there, it's like a horrifying flashback.

I stare at her frozen for a second. "What are you doing here?"

She takes a deep breath. "Come on, loser, I'm taking you to your fake prom."

I'm speechless. I step back so she can come in.

"Okay, listen, I can't take back what I did, okay? But I know I shouldn't have done it. I was just … *so* pissed. And it fucking hurt finding out how you feel about me." She sighs and looks off to the side. "But I've been thinking a lot about how I must come off, and it's not great."

I'm frankly stunned. I've never heard Cherri even come close to apologizing to anyone or having the slightest amount of self-awareness or self-reflection. When I don't say anything, she continues. "I guess you don't want to be around people because of what I did. And it's also really shitty what Chris did to you, and that's part of why you don't want to go. But I don't feel like you should be the one who can't go to, like, the big gay social event of the year because of us. You're the least to blame of everybody, so why should you get punished the most?"

Now she looks me in the eye. "I know you were afraid to go to the dance because you thought I would try to stop you or make fun of you, and I know that's why you kept things secret. I don't know if we can ever get back to being friends—if you'll ever be friends with me again—but let me do this one thing for you. Will you go with me?"

I've never heard her sound so unsure of herself, and suddenly I feel my anger toward her drain away.

"Okay, fine, loser. Let's do this fake prom."

"Thank fucking god!" Cherri sighs loudly and pulls out a little flask. "I brought vodka to keep me entertained while you make yourself pretty."

I jump in the shower, fix my hair, and pull out a couple different outfit options. Cherri helps me sort through them. "I kind of think this, under a suit coat." She holds up a glittery tank top. "And skinny pants and maybe those boots." I go with her idea. It is perfect, I have to admit, riding the line between dressy and campy. I even put on a little eyeliner. I'm actually feeling slightly excited to go.

Cherri drives us in her car. She's tapping the steering wheel the whole time, and I wonder if something else is going on. Finally she speaks.

"I feel so terrible about what I did. You know, everybody's got something they're hiding. It isn't abnormal or anything. And compared with a lot of other things, your secret was pretty, like, innocuous."

"Yeah." I don't want to get into it too much with her but, in the end, nothing really happened to my family. After a while, there was actually some backlash against the negativity. It turns out a lot of people are sympathetic to hoarders. Maybe it even made our family a little more relatable to people who'd just thought of us as rich privileged snobs.

Cherri continues. "There's other things people hide that are way worse."

"Yeah, I guess so."

"Yeah." She sighs. "So, over the break I found out my dad is in, like, a lot of trouble."

"How so?"

"It's … maybe kind of like a Ponzi scheme?" She shakes her head. "I don't know all the details, but it's really bad. I think he might be going to jail." Her voice breaks a little bit. "Nobody knows yet except you, Benji. But it doesn't really matter if you tell people or not, because it's gonna be coming out really soon. It's going to be everywhere. I don't even know what my mom and I are gonna do."

She draws in a shuddering breath. "Enjoy this ride tonight, girl, because I feel like if the feds don't take my car, we'll probably have to sell it anyway."

"Holy shit." *That* really puts my problems into perspective. "Shit, I'm so sorry."

"Well, one thing I'm glad of is that absolutely nobody is going to remember your parents' thing once this hits the news." She looks over at me. "I don't know if you'll believe me, but I was trying to think of a way to make things up to you even before I found out about my dad. This isn't what made me realize what a massive bitch I've been—I'd already figured that out."

"Chill, girl, I believe you." I try to keep my tone light even though I'm on the verge of tears.

"Thanks." She tosses her hair back. "Anyway, let's try to forget about that, because there's absolutely nothing I can do about it and I just wanna have a fucking dramatic time tonight! So what's our plan—how do we feel about Jemma? How many drinks should I throw on her? What if Chris is there—should I kneecap him?"

We both crack up. "Let's just be spontaneous and see what happens."

Cherri and I get waved in by the teacher manning the school entrance. I realize I never bought a ticket, but they're selling them at the gym door, so I pay for me and Cherri.

There's a small crowd, but more and more people are coming in, so it won't be for long. I take our coats and hang them up. As I wander back across the room looking for Cherri, I run into Alicia, of all people. We wave hesitantly at each other.

"Hey Benji!" She gestures to a guy next to her. "Um, have you met Emilio?"

"I don't think so." I hold my hand out and he shakes it. "Great to meet you."

He smiles and returns the greeting in a soft voice, and I can instantly see why Alicia couldn't resist him.

I start to leave, and Alicia walks with me a little way. "I figured this would be a more chill place than homecoming or prom to, like, just give him a shot." She giggles a little nervously. "Is, uh, anyone else here?"

I know what she means. "Yeah, Cherri's here." Her eyes get a little bigger. "But I think she's gonna be a little more chill from now on." Alicia looks curious but relieved.

"Are you having a good time?" I glance back toward Emilio.

She brightens. "Oh my god, yes. He's so sweet and sooo hot."

I can't help but smile. "I'm so happy for you!"

"Thanks Benji!" Her face clouds over. "How are you doing?"

"You know what? Not too bad!" And I actually mean it.

I find Cherri and we make a slow circuit of the room. We come across Alicia and Emilio again and I can tell how surprised Alicia is by her transformation.

We pass by Jemma fixing some drooping streamers. She spots me as she climbs off the step stool. I lift my hand and she waves back. I wonder how she's been holding up after everything, and I realize I don't feel mad at her at all.

CHAPTER TWENTY-FOUR: JEMMA

Monica was right. Once I stop feeling so
defensive, I realize no one in the GSA is being
hostile or avoiding me. I'd normally be stressed
out as the dance gets closer, but just the relief
of not feeling like an outcast anymore does
wonders for my nerves as we get everything
set up.

When it's almost time to open the doors, I
take my dress to the bathroom and get
changed. It's an ankle-length navy blue
sequined gown that clings to my body. I
remember picking it out over a month ago,

imagining taking Chris to the dance, and that makes me a little sad, but not nearly as bad as I used to feel when I thought about him.

I walk back into the gym. Some GSA members catch sight of me, and they cheer and whistle. I laugh and do a little turn, blowing kisses like some kind of fifties bombshell. It starts to feel like a party already, even though the gym is mostly empty. We get the music going and all the early people are laughing and talking, and then more people start arriving a few at a time, and at one point Monica leans over and whispers to me. "It's working!" We grab each other's hands and do an excited little dance.

I wander the gym, checking on decorations, keeping the snack table somewhat tidy, and just watching people have fun and feeling good that I was a big part in making that happen.

At one point I see Benji pass by. That's surprising enough on its own, but he's with Cherri and that's even more surprising. Most shocking of all, for once I feel like she's not already judging everything.

The gym keeps filling up, and I see a few of the people on the dance floor are hetero couples, but not all of them. It's exactly what we were going for—an all-inclusive dance.

On one wall, a whiteboard is slowly filling up with names. Instead of having a prom king and queen we're going to elect two monarchs of whatever gender, and rather than making it a big complicated thing, people can just write whoever they want. I'm standing on the sidelines, just floating with happiness and relief, when I see Benji coming over, without Cherri this time. He stands next to me.

"Hey, Jemma."

"Hey! Thanks for coming. I wasn't sure you were, you know, sold on this idea."

"Yeah, I guess not. But I've been thinking about things differently these days. Cherri too; she's the one who talked me into coming." That is genuinely surprising. Benji sighs and looks up at the ceiling like he's trying to gather his courage for something. "So … can we talk about what happened?"

I thought maybe that's why he came over, but it still feels big and weird to have those words hanging in between us. "Sure." Even a couple hours ago I might've hesitated more, but I truly do feel like a lot of my bitterness over the situation is gone. And most of it wasn't really directed at Benji in the first place.

"I'm not mad anymore, and I was never very upset with you." I marvel at how his words mirror my thoughts so closely. "I'm honestly just really curious about how you and Chris got together and how all that went down."

I have to admit, he's not the only one who's been wondering about that. So we compare notes, and we discover it was only a couple days apart that we each first kissed Chris (and that we both initiated it). It turns out that Benji had wanted to keep what he was doing with Chris quiet too, although for different reasons than me.

It makes me look at everything in a whole different way. "I wonder how it made him feel, having two people interested in him but both of them wanting to hide it."

"Confused, I bet." Benji looks a little sad. "Maybe like we were embarrassed to be seen with him or something, you know?"

"Yeah." Something else occurs to me. "And also like neither of us were taking him seriously as, like, a boyfriendish type of person." Benji laughs at the made-up word but seems to get what I'm saying. "And I was still kind of messing around with Monica," I add.

"And I had this thing with Lance; it pretty much stopped once Chris and I started getting together, but it was still out there as an option; I never said I'd stop seeing him or anything."

"God. It really was a whole big clusterfuck, wasn't it? And not all of it is his fault."

Benji nods. "Honestly, when I think about it, the main reason I freaked out is because I guess I started feeling a lot more for Chris than I ever meant to. But I never told *him* that."

"Same!" The similarities are kind of crazy. "Literally the first time I talked about my feelings or even went anywhere in public with him was that night you caught us kissing."

We're silent for a bit, processing that. "It was a really weird situation," Benji says finally, "but I don't see any reason we shouldn't be friends, right?"

I hesitate only a second before I agree. "We can be the Chris Quinn Survivors Support Group."

I look across the room and freeze. I swear to god it's like we conjured him or something, because there Chris is, standing in the doorway to the gym. Beside him his friend Marty elbows him and says something in his ear that makes him laugh. My heart flutters when I see his face light up like it used to.

I lean my head toward Benji. "Do you see that?"

"Yeah." He sounds just as shocked as I feel.

"That's one ballsy guy." I laugh. "I mean I'm not mad at him anymore really, and it sounds like you're not much either, but in everyone else's eyes, he's the guy who fucked over two of the most well-known gay people in the school."

"God, you're right. Good for him for coming."

"Agreed." I look away, mostly because I don't want anyone to catch me staring at Chris and think I'm about to start a scene or anything like that.

The dance just flies by after that and then it's the halfway point, time to start voting for the monarchs. Monica and I head to the whiteboard.

There are ten or so names scrawled on the whiteboard, about an equal mix of boys and girls. I see Benji's name right at the very top. A couple lines down I see my name. And down at the bottom, like some weird sick joke—which it probably is—somebody has scrawled "Chris Quinn."

I glance at Monica, who looks worried. "What do you want to do, Jemma?"

I don't know whether I'm more pissed or embarrassed or an equal combination of the two. But in light of all the weirdness in my life over the past couple months, it actually doesn't shock me too terribly much. "Looks like some asshole decided to inject a little drama into our voting process. It sucks, but I think we should just do what we said we were gonna do. These are the nominees, so we'll see what happens."

Monica nods slowly. "I'll get Brianna to help me with the announcement since you're one of the nominees." She smiles tentatively. "You sure you're okay?"

"I'm fine." It's nice to be able to say that in all honesty. "You've helped me so much. I don't know how I'd feel if you hadn't been so cool this afternoon, but now I honestly feel like I can handle anything."

She squeezes my hand. "Okay."

She and Brianna step up onto the stage. Another GSA member turns down the music as they approach the microphone. The crowd noise drops down to whispers and all eyes turn to them.

Brianna speaks first. "Hi everybody, thanks for coming to Hennepin High's very first queer prom!" She and Monica smile as the room bursts into applause. Then Brianna holds her hands up. "So now we're going to announce the nominees for our monarchs! Just to let you know the rules, there's no king and no queen, so anybody of any gender or sexuality can be one of our two winners." There's a shorter round of applause and murmurs of anticipation. Monica glances at the list she copied down from the whiteboard. "We're going to ask our nominees to come up when their name is called so everyone can get a good look at them before we hand out ballots," she says. "And your nominees are … Benji Swenson!"

There are some gasps. I look over at Benji and he was clearly unaware his name was on the whiteboard, but Cherri, standing next to him, nudges him and smiles a little too knowingly. I wonder if she put him on the list. After hesitating he shrugs, smiles back at her, and walks up onto the stage to cheers.

Monica keeps going down the list. My name comes up and I step onto the stage too. After a few more people are called up, the last name Monica says is Chris's. All eyes in the room turn to him, and the chatter in the gym drops to near silence. I see a familiar flush creeping over his face. I really feel for him in this moment. He looks like he wants to bolt out of the room, but Marty puts an arm around his shoulder and gives him a reassuring squeeze. He drags his feet up to the stage and stands at the end of the line with his eyes glued to the floor.

Monica continues as if nothing dramatic has happened. "Okay, let's have one more round of applause for all of our beautiful nominees! Nominees, wave and smile so they'll see what charming monarchs you can be." Feeling like an idiot, I give a little wave and a smirk. "Okay, we'll let you guys go while we pass out ballots."

I leave the stage with relief only a few people behind Benji. He turns around and gives me a "what the fuck is this shit" look. I shrug and spread my arms wide.

We meet up in a corner of the gym. "Can you fucking believe that just happened?" he whispers. "I know Cherri put my name on there but what the fuck—all three of us?"

"I'm pretty sure someone in the GSA put mine up, so the real question is what sick fuck decided to put Chris on the spot like that?"

"Oh god, it could've been anyone dying to start some drama."

"Yeah, you're right." Just then the crowd parts a little bit and I almost gasp. Chris is heading straight for us. "Benji," I mutter.

He looks in the direction I'm staring. "Wow. I guess people are going to get the big scene they wanted."

Before I can answer, Chris is standing in front of us, hands shoved in his pockets. Despite the pretty sharp suit he's got on, he looks like a little kid who knows he's in trouble. "Hey Jemma, hey Benji."

"Hi," we accidentally say in near unison.

"Umm …" Chris hesitates and scrubs his hand across his face in a way I know so well. "I'm sorry this happened. Someone's just trying to embarrass us, I guess."

"You think?" I can tell Benji is being playful, but Chris lowers his eyes like he's been told off.

"Yeah. Well, I'm gonna head out, but … before I go I hoped you would let me apologize. There's no excuse for what I did," he adds hastily, "but if you'd just let me …"

"Go ahead, Chris," I say.

"Thank you." He takes a deep breath. "I—I knew what I was doing was probably wrong, but it all started so weirdly, I just—" He stops, shakes his head, and starts over.

"I'd literally never been involved with anyone before this. I was clueless, and you both just came out of the blue for me, like magic, and I told myself as long as it wasn't serious it was probably all right to go along with it. I mean I figured you'd probably get sick of me pretty quick."

He laughs without humor. "And then when things started to feel serious it was, like, too late. I didn't know how to tell either of you without sounding like an asshole and hurting your feelings. And, well, I figured if I said anything, neither of you would wanna be with me anymore. And so I kept putting it off because I didn't want that to happen."

He looks up. "Benji, I really really like you." I can't help but feel a jealous twinge in my stomach when I hear that. But then Chris turns his eyes to me. "Jemma, I like you so much." He stares at his feet again. "I liked you both the whole time, and I still do. I guess what I wanted to say is … I'd never be able to stop liking either one of you. Not that you're asking me to choose or that you even wanna hear this or care what I think about anything, but I just wanted you to know that I really did like you, and I still like you, and I guess I'm gonna keep on liking you." He scuffs the floor with his shoe. Then more words come out in a rush.

"I'm gonna get out of here so you don't have to feel awkward, and I'm gonna leave you guys alone from now on. You don't have to worry about me. I know you want nothing to do with me and I don't blame you. So that's all I wanted to say. Have a great rest of your night. Thank you for listening to me."

Before either of us can say anything, Chris hurries away. Marty catches up with him, says something, and leans in to listen to Chris, then puts his arm around him and accompanies him out the door.

Benji and I don't know what to do next. It's so much to take in.

Someone comes by handing out ballots. We each take one along with a stubby little eraserless pencil. I think about it and then I write down two people's names—not mine or Benji's or Chris's—and shove my vote into the ballot box.

A few minutes later, when everyone's had a chance to vote, a couple GSA members count the ballots in a corner of the gym.

The music dies down as Brianna takes center stage again. "All right, we have our winners!" The crowd gets quiet.

"And your queer prom monarchs are …" She opens a folded piece of paper. Her eyes widen just for a second before she tries to look normal. "Jemma Matthews and Benji Swenson!"

There's a moment of shocked silence, but then a few GSA members start clapping and squealing, and soon everyone joins in. Benji and I look at each other in disbelief, but the applause keeps going, so we finally walk up to the podium to get our plastic crowns.

"Do we get to have a first dance?" Benji smirks at me.

"Oh yeah. It was always our plan to humiliate whoever won. I guess I should've thought that one through, huh?"

He laughs. A slow song starts playing and I grab his hand and lead him down to the middle of the floor, where the crowd parts for us. We start dancing with exaggerated dignity, cracking each other up as we stare into each other's eyes. "Do you think this is the drama that they wanted?" I whisper.

Benji snorts. "I think whichever of these fuckers tried to start something are feeling really let down right about now." He twirls me around as other couples join the dance around us.

CHAPTER TWENTY-FIVE: CHRIS

The nursing home is quieter and more deserted than it was the day my family came here around Christmas. The decorations have mostly been taken down and everything is a depressing beige color. Old cooking smells fill the air, making me feel a little nauseous.

It's just me today. I check in at the front desk and tell the nurse I know my way to my grandpa's room.

I couldn't sleep basically at all after the dance, and weirdly enough, after a while, I stopped fixating on Benji and Jemma and thought about Grandpa instead. It hit me that, even though it might not help him if I visit, there's *no* chance I can help if I don't. I need to stop being selfish and start being there for him the way he always was for me.

I build up my resolve and knock on his door. There's no answer, of course, so I walk in anyway and shut the door behind me. There's no lock on the inside, which makes sense. So I can't guarantee we'll have privacy for what I'm about to try. Oh well.

Grandpa is slumped in his wheelchair by his bed. A bouquet of wilting flowers sits in a vase. Grandma probably brings them every couple of days. Photos are taped up on the walls around him: Pictures of him and Grandma from their wedding day and other times when they were young, as well as some more recent ones. Me and my brother and sister at different ages. Pictures of my dad ranging from when he was a kid to now, and photos of the whole family. The most recent one was taken around Christmas a year ago. We never did get around to one this Christmas.

Grandpa's staring down at his lap, not saying anything. There's a little bit of drool in the corner of his mouth. I feel a combination of pity and an overwhelming urge to run away. Which I probably could; he's not even looking at me. But instead I sit on his bed next to his wheelchair. "Hi Grandpa." He doesn't look up. "It's Chris. It's your grandson." No response.

I keep talking anyway. I talk to him about school a little bit. I tell him about Jemma and Benji. I know he's not listening or understanding anything, so it actually feels like a safe place to talk about my feelings. After a while, when he still barely looks aware that someone's there, I pull out my phone and open YouTube.

"You remember this, Grandpa?" I hit play on The Drifters singing "Save the Last Dance for Me." I consider talking about the last time we heard it, when we were hanging out on his back porch. But instead, I just let the music ring out through the room. Slowly, Grandpa's head lifts a little bit. I look down and I see his hand tapping the arm of the wheelchair. He starts humming the melody under his breath.

"This was you and Grandma's song—Margaret. This was you and Margaret's song." He lifts his eyes to me but I can't tell if he understands what I'm saying, and his head starts to droop again. As the song comes to an end, I hit replay. Then I reach into my coat pocket for one more thing. I absolutely know I'm going to get in deep shit and maybe get kicked out for what I'm about to do, but I have to try it anyway.

I strike a match and light the cigarillo. I take a couple of puffs, grimacing but managing not to take any into my lungs this time at least. My gums tingle the way I remember from the last time. With my free hand, I waft some of the smoke in Grandpa's direction.

And suddenly his blue eyes snap into focus, clear and lucid. He looks right at me, and he smiles. I can't believe it. I take another puff and blow a little more smoke towards him, and he speaks for the first time this whole visit. "He used to smoke those all the time." I don't get it though—is he talking about himself in the third person?

"You mean *you* did, Grandpa?"

He cocks his head curiously and looks at me. "I mean Theodore."

"Oh, right." I say it to encourage him to keep talking, even though I have no idea who he's talking about. A friend from college, or maybe farther back, one of the bad kids he hung out with in elementary school and used to tell me hilarious stories about. "Who's Theodore again?"

"I really developed a taste for them because of him." Grandpa's voice is strange, faraway. "Margaret couldn't stand them, so I only smoked around Theo." So it was someone he knew at the same time as Grandma. I think that would've been college or maybe after.

The song comes to an end and I hit play a third time. Grandpa smiles again. "This was one of our songs, me and Margaret."

"I know." He looks off into an invisible distance again. I don't want him to sink into the past, but it feels different now. Not like he thinks he's really there, but like he's remembering clearly. I hope. "Tell me more about that."

"She played it for me to let me know we belong together. No matter what I did."

It's funny, but I'd pictured Grandma being the one flirting with guys when Grandpa first told me this was their song. I guess maybe *he* played the field a little bit when he and Grandma were together.

I'm still trying to piece it all together when Grandpa says, "I knew I couldn't have them both."

"What?"

"I knew I couldn't have them both forever. Especially not Theo. It just wasn't done back then. It would've been too hard for him. And for me, I guess." Grandpa looks thoughtful. "And I loved Margaret. But it was hard to admit it had to end."

I think through what he's saying. He can't possibly mean what I'm thinking he means. "Who is Theo?" I ask again. He looks at me with that same quizzical look as before.

"You don't know." He sounds a little surprised. "Well, I suppose we kept it a pretty good secret." He smiles. "Theo was my first love." His lip quivers and tears start to gather in his eyes. "And Margaret is my last love." His voice is raspy. "I was lucky to fall in love twice. Not everybody gets that." He swallows. "I didn't feel too lucky, though, at the time. Sometimes I wished he and I had never met, so we'd never have to say goodbye." He starts humming again, then stops.

"I hope you find love, Chris." It's the first time he's acknowledged even knowing who I am this whole time. I should be thrilled, but I'm more caught up in figuring out what he's talking about. "But I hope you don't have to hurt anyone like I did."

Just then there's a banging on the door and someone flings it open. "What is going on here?" A nurse storms into the smoke-filled room.

I look around frantically for a place to put out the cigarillo. "Sorry!" I toss it in a half-empty plastic cup on Grandpa's night table. It hisses and goes out as the lit end hits the water. "I'm really sorry."

The nurse grabs the cup angrily. "I am going to have to ask you to leave, but first you're coming with me to the office while I report this incident." I look over at Grandpa as the song fades out again, and I turn off my phone. His head is drifting back down toward his chest, and he looks almost like he did when I first got here. But I swear I see a little smile playing around his lips, and the tears on his cheeks haven't fully dried yet, so I know it really happened.

I leave the nursing home, calling Grandma to make sure she's home. The first thing I do when I get there is explain the fiasco with the cigarillo and why I did it. She's not mad; in fact she laughs. "That was really smart actually. I'll try to smooth things over so you're not banned permanently."

"Thanks, Grandma. I'll try to bring other things to jog his memory that won't get me in so much trouble next time." When our laughter dies down, I take a deep breath.

"Grandma, I've been, like, keeping lots of secrets, and it's turned out really bad for me. So I need to know the truth." I can't believe what I'm about to say. "Before you were married, was Grandpa with someone else at the same time as you?"

She's at a loss for words, so I explain what Grandpa said. She sits me down and pours us some coffee. Then she starts talking.

Part of me had wondered if it was just something that Grandpa's scrambled brain was concocting out of thin air or mixed-up memories, but Grandma tells basically the same story. Not long after he and Grandma had started dating, she figured out that he and his best friend were more than that to each other.

"Once I confronted him, he was totally honest with me. He confessed everything. I know it was scary for him. A lot of girls probably would've left him or exposed him as a homosexual out of revenge, but—and maybe it's because I knew Theo too—I just couldn't do either. As shocked as I was, it made sense. I asked if he really loved me and he swore he did.

"I took some time to think about it all. And then I said he could keep seeing Theo and that I would keep seeing him too, as long as there were no more secrets or lies between us." She shakes her head. "If any of our friends had guessed, or our parents … but we were really careful."

My head is spinning; none of this is anything I ever expected to hear about my grandparents. "Weren't you jealous?"

She thinks about it. "I guess I was more shocked than anything at first. And then I did feel a little jealousy. But then I thought, what we have is special. Theo's not taking anything away from that. And I think Theo felt the same way about me. We each had something special. Grandpa took good care of me, and he treated Theo well too."

She grimaces. "But I did tell Grandpa at some point that if he wanted to make a family with me, we couldn't keep it up. I knew if he kept seeing him, someone would find out and it could destroy us all. And if we had kids, it could destroy them too.

"I didn't press it after that, but eventually he ended it. He didn't really talk or leave his room for weeks after that." She sighs. "I've never felt so guilty. But he had to. We had to let that friendship go, too. Grandpa knew he wouldn't be able to stand being around Theo and not being *with* him."

I think about that for the rest of the day. I think about having to tell Benji or Jemma that I can never be with them. Even though I can't be with either of them now, I still can't imagine ever rejecting one of them like that. Then I think about all the movies and books out there where someone falls in love with two people, and they always have to choose. I guess that's just the way it is. Grandpa must've realized that he couldn't keep being so selfish.

The next day is Sunday. I think about going back to school after the weekend is over and I don't feel as much dread as before. I know Jemma and Benji are probably still mad at me, but something about the way they were listening made me feel like at least they were hearing where I was coming from. Maybe over time they'll stop feeling hurt by what I did. I'll probably never know, but I hope so.

I don't see Jemma at all during the day on Monday. I see Benji in English class, of course. He gives me a sort of a neutral smile when I walk in. I smile back, grateful for anything that isn't the cold shoulder.

After school I'm waiting by my car for Marty when I get a text. I pull out my phone and my heart leaps into my throat. It's Jemma. "Can you come over to my house at four for an emergency GSA meeting?"

The first thing I wonder is, why is she inviting me to the GSA when she pretty much told me not to ever come back?

Then I start to worry; what else could've gone wrong at the dance after I left? That's the only thing I can think of that would cause the need for an emergency meeting.

I'm also confused about why the GSA isn't meeting in the usual classroom. But then I figure maybe since it's not the regular day, they can't get access to it.

I drop Marty off at his house and head over to Jemma's. My stomach is churning. I'm glad she wants my help, but what if whatever the problem is, it's somehow my fault? I can't imagine having to deal with even more guilt about something else I messed up.

Jemma comes to the door of her building. She says hi and smiles a little but doesn't say anything else, which makes me even more nervous. She leads me up to her place and into her living room. I see right away that no other members of the GSA are there.

But Benji is.

I can't read his expression. My stomach sinks. This might be an even worse problem than I could imagine. I feel like I'm entering the principal's office.

Jemma sits down next to Benji. She must sense how I feel because she says, "Mr. Quinn, we've brought you in here to discuss a very serious situation." Benji laughs. I don't know what to do or say, so I just stand there until Jemma points at a chair across from them.

Benji breaks the silence. "Did you know that we were elected monarchs at the dance?"

"No!" It surprises me that I didn't hear any gossip about that during the day.

"I think we bored everyone with how undramatic it was," Jemma says. She and Benji laugh together like they're sharing some inside joke. "But anyway, it gave me and Benji a chance to talk and realize that we want to be friends again."

"That's really great." I mean it, too. The thought that they got anything positive out of this whole mess makes me happy.

"We figured something else out too," Benji says.

"What?"

They exchange glances that I can't even begin to interpret. It feels like forever before they answer.

EPILOGUE: TRIO

Benji

The days are getting longer, so it's not quite dark out as I pull up to the curb and send a text. My phone dings a reply and a minute later, Chris comes down the walk. Picking his way through the icy slush, he gets in the passenger side.

"Hi." I smile, and give him a brief kiss. I can already sense how freaked out he is, so I inch my car down the block to a spot with no streetlight. As soon as I put it in park, Chris leans toward me and cups the back of my neck, and our lips meet again, lingering this time. He clearly wants to take his mind off what's coming.

I wish we could just skip the talent show and fool around in my car for hours, but I pull away reluctantly. "We'd better go. I don't want to make you late."

We hold hands as I drive, and his feels colder than usual. "What if I really really fuck up tonight? Like, bomb so bad that you're embarrassed to be associated with me?"

I park at our next destination and take both his hands in mine. "Listen to me. If your, like, worst-case scenario happens—I don't know what you're even imagining, that you'll accidentally go on stage in your underwear and then slip on a banana peel? Well, even if *that* happens, I'll still be proud to be your boyfriend, okay?" I kiss him again and shoo him out of the car. "Hurry up; we're running out of time!"

Jemma

Chris rings and I buzz him in. A minute later I meet him at the door of my place and pull him inside. He wraps me in his long arms as we kiss. He hasn't lost his puppydog eagerness but he's gotten *really* good at kissing.

It hits me all over again, as it still does from time to time, that this is a very strange situation to be in, especially for someone who thought she was a lesbian most of her life. And yet, as weird as it is, it feels more natural and right than any relationship I've had before.

I push Chris away gently. "We shouldn't keep Benji waiting." I grab my lipstick from my purse and hurry to the bathroom mirror.

Chris follows and watches from the doorway. "I can't even believe how pretty you are."

I pretend to be stern, even though my heart skips a beat. "Stop it. I am *not* making out with you again now that I've got my lipstick on. Now let's go."

Chris

The backstage of the auditorium is filled with an odd assortment of people in costumes with props and instruments, humming to themselves, rehearsing lines, practicing dance moves and magic tricks.

"This is crazy." My stomach is churning. I look at myself in a mirror, fiddling with my hair, tugging at my shirt. Everything I do just makes me look like more of a mess.

Jemma laughs. "No more than a lot of other things that've happened this year. Anytime this seems too crazy, think about some other crazy shit we've been through and you'll feel like this is the most normal thing you've ever done."

"It's true." Benji straightens my collar and runs his fingers through my hair, somehow instantly making me look a lot better. "Soon it'll be over and we can celebrate!"

"And if it all goes to hell," Jemma adds, "we'll just drown our sorrows together. How's that?"

I try to laugh. I'm still freaked the fuck out, but all their fussing over me is so sweet, I do feel a little better.

"How about brunch tomorrow?" she says.

"Can't, I'm hanging out with Grandpa all morning." I don't always get a breakthrough like I did that first time I saw him in the home, but sometimes his old self kind of reappears, so I want to keep trying. I know it won't last forever, so I just make the most of it while I can.

"And I'm taking Mom to therapy," Benji says. "She's been saying she might be ready to start getting rid of things, so we might do that a little bit too." He shrugs. "I'm not getting my hopes up *too* much, but it makes me think maybe someday I could move back home again."

"I mean, as long as you keep your place for, like, all the orgies and stuff, right?" teases Jemma.

Benji nods fervently. "Oh yeah, you know I'm all about the orgies!"

A couple of kids passing by hear that and pause, looking at us and then each other with raised eyebrows. I feel my cheeks getting hot, but Jemma smirks. "It's what people think anyway. We can't stop them."

"Maybe tomorrow night at my place?" Benji says. "We can get drunk, play some games … Or have an orgy, I guess."

I know my face is bright red now, which makes Jemma laugh. "When will you stop blushing at every vaguely sexual thing anyone says?"

"Or, we can work on your midterm application a little," Benji adds.

Jemma groans. "Ugh, buzzkill." But she's still smiling a little.

The overhead lights blink off and on several times. The drama teacher shouts above the noise. "The show starts in five minutes, so I need everyone to quiet down back here. And anyone who's not part of an act needs to get out. Now." She looks severely at my girlfriend and boyfriend. My stomach still does somersaults when I even think those words.

Benji gives my collar one more pat, then stands back and looks me up and down. "You're gonna do great. And don't worry—if people don't laugh at your jokes, maybe they'll laugh at *you*. It's the same result either way, when you think about it."

That cracks me up despite my rising not-quite-panic. "Thanks." I squeeze his hand. He kisses me quickly.

I turn to Jemma. She stands on tiptoes to give me a kiss, then wipes my mouth with her thumb. "Sorry, lipstick."

The teacher storms back through. "All right, I mean it. Everybody out!"

I smile nervously at them, wishing they didn't have to go. "You guys will still like me either way, right? No matter how it turns out?"

"Promise." Benji touches my cheek and kisses me one more time, then grabs Jemma's hand and pulls her along as they hurry out to find seats.

ACKNOWLEDGMENTS

It's been a long time since I was in high school myself. Luckily my kids, Vee and Astrid, reviewed my manuscript and gave honest feedback that helped shape a more authentic, relatable narrative. As a soon-to-be high schooler, a keen observer of life, and an avid reader of YA fiction, Astrid lent me her expertise through several more rounds of revisions. I'm so grateful to both of them for their support and encouragement.

www.ingramcontent.com/pod-product-compliance
Lightning Source LLC
Chambersburg PA
CBHW051129190726
48290CB00006B/1765